Where did Holly McCade fit into his life?

Colin pictured her as an angel from heaven. She'd taken the time to help him, to rescue a poor, helpless student when he'd been floundering.

And somehow, she'd known just what he needed.

She'd discovered his heart, compelled him to confront his own fears. And he'd discovered his destiny. How had she done that?

She was incredible. She brought out the best in him, and he thought he might be a good influence on her, as well. Was it his imagination, or did she shine a little brighter when she was in his company?

Colin didn't trust his head when he was around her. Or his heart.

Who knew if she might steal it clean away?

Books by Deb Kastner

Love Inspired

DEB KASTNER

is the wife of a Reformed Episcopal minister, so it was natural for her to find her niche in the Christian/Inspirational romance market. She enjoys tackling the issues of faith and trust within the context of a romance. Her characters range from upbeat and humorous to (her favorite) dark and brooding heroes. Her plots fall anywhere between, from a playful romp to the deeply emotional.

When she's not writing, she enjoys spending time with her husband and three girls and, whenever she can manage, attending regional dinner theater and touring Broadway musicals.

The Christmas Groom
Deb Kastner

Published by Steeple Hill Books™

STEEPLE HILL BOOKS

Steeple
Hill™

ISBN 0-373-87202-X

THE CHRISTMAS GROOM

Copyright © 2002 by Debra Kastner

This edition published by arrangement with Steeple Hill Books.

® and TM are trademarks of Steeple Hill Books, used under license. Trademarks indicated with ® are registered in the United States Patent and Trademark Office, the Canadian Trade Marks Office and in other countries.

Visit us at www.steeplehill.com

Printed in U.S.A.

Therefore if the Son makes you free,
you shall be free indeed.

—*John* 8:36

To the LORD my God,
with grateful thanks.

Chapter One

Colin Brockman was late to his first day of school. More accurately, his first day *back* in school.

He crept as casually and quietly as his big, squeaky-tennis-shoed feet would let him into the muted twilight tones of his Child Psych auditorium classroom. Gym shoes were far more comfortable than navy dress shoes, but Colin found that, for a moment, he missed the familiarity of the spit and polish, the recognizable click of the heels as he walked.

At least he knew what to expect from navy issue. He hadn't a clue what to expect from this day.

With a relieved huff, he slid into a seat that, while made with an adult in mind, certainly didn't take into account his considerably large frame. He shifted backward and forward, left to right, knocking his knees against the bottom of the desk, raking his elbows against the steel hardware and knowing that with every movement he continued to draw unwanted attention to himself and his dilemma.

Didn't these desks adjust for height somehow? Or had he just picked one meant for a third-grade kid?

When no bolts loosened under his fingers, he changed tactics, turning, stretching and curving himself as smoothly as possible into the seat, mentally comparing himself to a piece of artist's molding clay.

Mashed, rolled and squished into the creation of the Master's form.

Despite his discomfort, Colin grinned at the mental picture he'd created of God pounding and kneading him into shape, and knew he wasn't so very far off. He was a work in progress, potter's clay in the Master's hands. He trusted God could make more of him than he could of himself—he'd gone that route already, and anyone with an eye could see where that had taken him.

He continued his slow, steady movements until he was certain he could breathe and stretch his long legs, which appeared to be his two greatest problems at the moment. That, and maybe the ability to actually reach the desk with his hand in case he wanted to take notes on a class that was rapidly moving along without him.

Pushing the hood of his oversize gray sweatshirt off his head with both palms, he used his fingers to scrub through the tips of his fine blond hair. It had been years since he'd grown his hair above a military buzz cut, and no one had mentioned how terribly it would itch and bother him.

Still, he thought he might live through it if he could grow it past the Chia Pet stage.

He smothered another grin. He didn't mind, not really. In the big scheme of things, it was a pretty small annoyance. At least he had the choice of whether or not to grow his hair out, to make his own decision about something even as minimal as that, for a change.

The navy, for all its many benefits, didn't give a man many choices, and Colin was eager to make up for lost time now that he was his own man.

Eager to begin his career as a student, he jammed one hand into his backpack, digging for a fresh spiral notebook and a pen or a pencil to write with. He was positive they were to be found somewhere in the depths of his bag.

Or at least thought they were there.

He was almost certain.

He bit the corner of his lip and made another pass at it. His hand closed over several items, which he grasped and discarded—a fork, a sock without a mate, a baseball, a stud finder he'd been using earlier in the day on his apartment wall in order to hang pictures.

He cringed, squeezing his eyebrows down close around his eyes as he called himself every kind of idiot. It was his first day of school. Surely he had remembered to throw in something to write on. And to write with.

At length, he found the notebook he wanted, but his blue ballpoint pen, the one he'd purchased especially for this new school year, eluded him, until he remembered suddenly he'd shoved it into the back left pocket of his jeans before he left.

So he wouldn't forget where it was, naturally.

Settling restlessly in his seat, he took a moment to look around, tapping his newly found pen on the top of his notebook as a rich female voice resonated warmly from the front of the room, speaking of classroom procedures, what to expect from the course and what homework assignments would be like.

Colin listened with only half an ear. He knew he should be paying more attention, especially on his first day, but he was more interested in his fellow students than what was going on at the front of the room.

Who were these people, and what were they in for? He didn't expect to fit in with a crowd of kids coming straight from high school, exactly, but...

Oh, man.

Old man was more like it. Was he really ready for this?

He was astounded at the profusion of young men in baggy pants, young ladies with fuchsia and other Easter colors striped in their hair, ill-concealed Game Boys peeking out of pockets, coats, dresses and purses. Bodies of both genders were pierced in places Colin didn't even want to think about.

Oh, man.

Where were the people like him? Where were the people who hadn't figured out they needed to go to school until they were—what was a nice way of phrasing it?—well past their adolescent prime?

Looking around him, he felt worlds older than the youngsters in this class, though that was hardly the truth. He was thirty, which wasn't exactly over the hill.

He was probably only a decade older than most of the students. But in experience, he was an antique compared to the young men and women sitting around him.

Or at least he felt that way.

His gaze wandered down to the floor of the auditorium, where a couple of professors, young ladies, were taking turns speaking. The muted sunlight made it hard to see that far down, but Colin's vision was excellent.

He smiled as his gaze shifted from one of the female professors to the other and riveted upon her.

He was much closer in age to that pretty little parcel with the gorgeous long legs, sashaying back and forth in the front of the room.

Much closer.

He didn't know why he hadn't noticed the attractive twenty-something woman earlier. He had to be really nervous to have missed that bright beacon of light in an otherwise shadowed room, for it was her warm voice lighting up the darkness.

And to think he hadn't even looked to the front of the room until now! Not to look for potential assignments or anything. He hadn't even glanced at the prominent overhead projector illuminating the middle of the room.

To think he'd almost continued on blissfully unaware of the lovely angel who would most certainly transform this class into something, if not pleasurable, then at least palatable.

He grinned. He couldn't help it if he liked a pretty face. He hadn't seen enough of them in the navy. His ambition to become a chaplain didn't make him blind to a pair of pretty eyes or make him immune to the scent of a beautiful woman.

He might not have a lot of relationship experience of his own to draw from, but he'd been around. He'd been there to watch firsthand when his beloved twin sister fell for the love of her life. He knew how it worked.

And to be honest, he wouldn't mind so very much if *it* worked on him.

In his opinion, God had saved the best for last. Women were the highlight of God's creative efforts, and when He'd finished Eve, He'd had good reason to pronounce His work *very good.*

He tossed his pen down on the desk and leaned

forward in his seat, intent on a better view. Now that he'd noticed the pretty prof, he couldn't take his eyes off her.

She had long, thick dark brown hair that gleamed with red highlights as it shifted when she walked. And her eyes were a dark, rich green, and the color of Christmas velvet.

Her sharp gaze was, he noticed with a blast of electric shock, pinned directly on him. He had no doubt whatsoever that she hadn't missed his tardy entrance to his first class on his first day of school, or of his subsequent fidgeting around in his seat as he unsuccessfully attempted to get settled.

He cleared his throat aloud.

That could be a problem.

She was obviously his teacher.

His *professor,* he mentally corrected. This was college, not grade school.

Miss Prof. Or was that *Mrs.?*

He flashed her his most charming grin. Surprise flashed across her gaze and her pretty, full lips hinted softly at a grin; but then the moment was gone. She frowned and lifted one eyebrow in silent question.

What was he up to?

He swore he saw the corners of her sweet lips twitch as she shook her head, looking put out and disappointed in that unique way elementary school teachers had of making their students feel guilty for misbehaving in their classroom.

Colin's back went up in a moment, his spine stiffening in stubbornness. If she was looking to make someone feel *guilty,* she was looking at the wrong student. This wasn't elementary school, and he wasn't a child anymore. He was paying good money to attend the seminary, and to take these university classes on the side.

This was his planet, his continent, his day, hour, minute, and he wasn't even counting seconds.

He was here because he wanted to be, and he'd arrive and leave when he wanted. He wouldn't purposely do anything to disrupt the class or bother any other students, but he wouldn't hand over any of his freshly minted independence, either.

He knew his philosophy sounded a good deal like a bad attitude, but it wasn't. He happily extended his generous outlook to the rest of the world, if they wanted it, which he very much doubted. He'd always thought himself a bit of a maverick.

In truth, he just wanted to find out what it meant to be footloose and fancy-free. He'd never had the chance to do that, even in his youth. And now that he had the time and opportunity, he wasn't going to give it up, even to a pretty professor.

He turned his attention to the first lecture, scribbling illegible notes on the first clean, crisp page of his notebook.

Colin was soon lost in thought and note-taking as he attempted to follow the lecture. Ms. *Gorgeous*

Legs—he clearly needed to find out her real name—was talking a mile a minute, and very animatedly, about something called the Hierarchy of Needs that some famous psychologist guy named Maslow had come up with.

Projected onto the screen at the front of the auditorium was a diagram in the shape of a triangle. A person, especially a child, the lovely woman explained, was unable to focus on obtaining or meeting the needs on the higher levels until he or she had fulfilled the lower-level needs, the base needs, if you will. Things such as finding food, warmth and shelter.

Colin frowned at the diagram he'd traced onto his paper. The more ethereal needs were indeed placed exclusively in higher rows.

But what about the search for God? Didn't that transcend even the most basic need barriers? As a future navy chaplain, he experienced the insatiable desire to know more, and quickly scribbled his own ideas in the margins.

Since he assumed he'd missed the part of the lesson on how the class was run, he wasn't certain how to go about getting his questions answered. He had no office hours or phone numbers to call.

"Serves you right, Brockman," he mumbled under his breath.

He started to raise his hand, then pulled it back down, deciding he'd ask his question at the end of the class...if he could remember it for that long.

There was a lot of stuff to think about, and this was only his first class of the day.

He'd always considered himself a smart man, but not necessarily good at book learning. If he was going to make it in college, he was going to have to apply himself, especially since he hadn't been to school in years.

"Your first assignment is going to feel like a big one," said the beautiful woman in the front of the room, her thick sable hair swishing hypnotically with each movement. Colin pressed his chin in his hand, scratching at the stubble. "But it's important that you take this project seriously, and have it completed by next Monday."

Colin paused in his note-taking and scowled, shaking his head in silent dissent.

"Great," he whispered under his breath. "A term paper on the very first week of school."

He was completely serious in his opposition, but the three-hundred-pound jock next to him bellowed out a deep-throated laugh.

"Something funny, gentlemen?" The sable-haired woman in the front of the room was eyeing him again. He bit his bottom lip against a smile. He really needed to learn her name.

"No, ma'am," he called out, and the boy next to him sniggered. Her lovely green eyes grazed over the younger man and landed squarely on Colin. Her gaze glimmered with amusement, though her posture was tight and her expression grim.

He resisted the urge to straighten his shoulders and couple his hands on the desk as he'd been taught to do in military school. Rather, he slid down in his seat just about as far as his large frame could fit.

Maybe his question could wait. Maybe he could simply disappear altogether.

"Your assignment," announced Holly McCade, deciding her best strategy on this first day of a new year of student teaching was simply to ignore the snickering, juvenile troublemakers in the back, "is simply this. Find somewhere you can observe a situation in which children are struggling to meet their basic needs. There are dozens of examples I could give you on where to find these children, but I leave that part up to your discretion and creativity. Please feel free to come see me for help and/or suggestions if you run into any trouble with this part of the assignment."

She paused, struggling, for a moment, with her phrasing. "You must observe those children for at least two hours, but the more time you spend with them, the better of an understanding you will walk away with."

She held up her own three-ringed notebook. "Taking notes would be a good idea, but you are not required to do so. You will be required to hand in a one-page paper telling me who you selected, where they are located and how much time you spent observing.''

''Is that all?'' asked a surprised young lady in the first row. The girl was obviously just out of high school. She was wearing too much makeup, and wore her boyfriend's high school letter jacket around her shoulders.

Holly laughed. ''Yes. That's all.''

A surreptitious glance at her watch signaled a frenzy of activity as students packed up their books and got their things together.

And she hadn't even said the word *go,* she thought, smothering another smile.

''Remember, if you have any questions, I'll be here for another ten minutes.''

A couple of students responded to that call. One obviously wanted to get in good with the teacher and make sure Holly knew who he was. The other was a typical overachiever obsessing about whether or not Holly would give an A+ on the assignment when the student in question was only allowed to turn in one page.

''Take it easy,'' said a rich, laughing baritone from somewhere behind Holly's left shoulder. ''You make it sound like you *want* her to make us write a term paper or something.''

''I...well...I...'' stammered the girl, and then picked up her books and darted out of the classroom without another word.

Somehow Holly instinctively knew to whom the voice belonged even before she turned around. She was certain it must be the man she'd noticed sitting at the top round of the auditorium. The man with sparkling blue eyes and an untidy bit of light blond hair.

It felt strange for her, as a student teacher, to be teaching someone older than she was, although the man could hardly be called her grandfather. She guessed him to be around thirty, only two years or so older. Not much of an age difference.

Older people returned to college all the time in this day and age. She'd taught a retired couple last semester and hadn't seen anything strange about that. So it wasn't such an oddity for this man to be enrolled in her class.

But it certainly felt like an oddity, especially when the character in question had spent the study hour cracking jokes with an eighteen-year-old boisterous jock. She would have thought a guy this man's age would have respect for the classroom, if not the teacher.

"Can I help you?" she asked testily.

His grin slipped. "To tell you the truth, ma'am, I don't know."

Was he toying with her? She searched his face, but saw no hint of his intentions. His expression gave her no clue whether he was serious or not.

But dealing with potential class clowns was part of

student teaching, and she sighed inwardly, even as she steeled herself to be graceful under adversity, no matter how handsome the package.

With effort, she smiled. "Do you have a question about the assignment?" she asked, rephrasing the query.

"Question, comment, statement," Colin said. "My name is Colin Brockman, by the way." He thrust out his hand with a wink and a grin.

He already knew her name, at least if he'd been paying attention in class. Since he probably hadn't been, and because she didn't want him to keep calling her *ma'am*, she responded.

"Holly McCade," she answered. She hadn't missed a beat in their conversation, but her heart missed several beats as she shook his hand. He had large palms, smooth fingers and a firm but gentle grip.

"My question has to do with that triangle thing you talked about in your lecture," he said.

"The Hierarchy of Needs," she supplied. "The one suggested by Dr. Maslow."

He nodded vigorously. "Well, the thing is, Miss… Mrs.…uh, Holly," he stammered, then stopped for a moment and tried again. "I believe there's a bigger base than the one you've—Dr. Maslow's—given."

Intriguing. He *had* been paying attention. "How do you mean?"

"I mean God, ma'am. I think there should be a new bottom row—one reserved for God alone."

Holly's heart stirred. As a Christian, she shared similar feelings, but of course could not teach those beliefs openly in a public classroom. Besides, Dr. Maslow's theory had been used in the psych classroom for years.

"Do you mean," she asked slowly, "in the place of eating and sleeping?"

He frowned and shook his head. "No."

"Please continue, Colin. Keep in mind that Maslow did make room for metaphysical thinking at higher levels of the triangle, addressed after the basic needs have been provided for."

His eyes narrowed in thought, and he stroked the stubbly line of his jaw. Shaving hadn't, apparently, been the reason he was late for class.

"The more I think about it, the more I wonder if God should really occupy a level at all," he said, sounding surprisingly contemplative, considering his scruffy appearance.

He continued, sounding more confident with each word. "God isn't a system, something you think about or organize with. He's not Someone you can compartmentalize or graph. I guess what I'm trying to say, and not very eloquently, is that I think He's a relationship. *Without* boundaries, or format. He transcends the triangle."

"Maybe He *is* the triangle," Holly suggested quietly. "By and in and through everything—every need, every want, every desire."

Before Holly could catch a breath, Colin pounded a nearby table with his fists and hooted with glee. "That's it! Hot diggity-dog."

She chuckled nervously, brushing her fingers through her hair as she covertly looked around to see if anyone had noticed his outburst. To her relief, the room was empty except for the two of them.

"Ain't life just grand?" he asked with a smile. "Don't you just love it when you *get it?*"

She'd never thought about it that way, but she supposed she did enjoy the thrill of discovery. His childlike enthusiasm was contagious, and she found herself smiling back at him.

And she found herself modifying her initial opinion of her unusual scholar. Colin might, after all, be precisely the type of student she wanted to teach. "Do you know where you're going to go for your assignment?" she blurted without thinking.

He shook his head, his blond hair fluffing out every which direction. He reminded her of a little boy growing out his summer haircut, or maybe of a wild turkey, she wasn't sure which.

Either way, he looked adorable.

"I have a couple of ideas, if you'd like to join me," she offered tentatively, unsure why she was reaching out to him. She wasn't sure she was supposed to be interacting with students on this level. She wasn't even sure she liked him.

"The Christian Relief Center is open to visitors. We could go there," she suggested.

"These are street people?"

"Yes. CRC caters to women on the street who are there due to divorce or battering. There are always lots of children to observe. CRC tries to sweep these women and children off the street and, well, meet their lower hierarchical needs."

"That's a mouthful," Colin said. "Hierarchical. Try saying that three times fast."

Holly felt the heat rush to her face. "You don't have to go with me if you have somewhere else to go."

His gaze flickered with amusement. He reached out and lightly chucked her under her chin. "I have no place else to go. Lead on, fair Holly, and I will follow."

Chapter Two

Holly McCade switched her position on the university park bench, crossing her left leg over her right and stretching her right arm across the back of the bench. She turned her head, taking in the landscape all the way around her. Colorado was gorgeous in the fall, and Greeley was no exception. Though it was too early for the aspen leaves to turn their traditional shades of yellow, orange and gold, the day was still vivid with color.

Greeley lay on the eastern plains, and Holly could see the green and brown patchwork of farmland and ranchland from where she sat. And though there were one or two taller buildings marring the view, she could even see the front range of the Rocky Mountains in all their majestic splendor, far enough away to require a plan, but close enough for a drive.

Students milled around between classes, talking, studying or playing Frisbee on the lawn. Birds chattered from the trees, and there was even a big brown squirrel helping himself to lunch from a convenient garbage barrel.

It was all very nice, and she might even have enjoyed the morning sunshine and the lovely views, except that she wasn't sitting here to spend half her Saturday watching university students play games and hungry squirrels rummage for food.

She was waiting for Colin Brockman.

With a loud sigh, she glanced at her watch.

Again.

She didn't know why she'd offered to do this— meet with a man she hardly knew and wasn't completely sure she liked. Probably she was under some misguided, philanthropic notion that she could help him broaden his horizons on his way to a better understanding of child psychology.

And to have waited over an hour for him—she must really be losing it. She wasn't the young woman with low self-esteem who'd do anything for a man she might have been in her youth. Anything but!

She should go. She could be busy with something else. Her time was important, and Colin obviously didn't respect that. Or respect her, for that matter.

She should have gone with her first impression, she decided. Colin was nothing more than an overgrown kid with mischief in his heart.

She suddenly recalled all those little things she noticed about him that clinched her first opinion—the cut of his uneven hair, the day's growth of beard on his face. Even his clothes looked like he'd thrown them on from where they'd once lay crumpled, probably on the floor of his bedroom.

He was a rascal, all right.

A *late* rascal.

Anger and frustration welled up inside her heart. Anger at herself. Why had she bothered waiting?

She sighed and reached for her bag. She already knew the answer to that question before she asked it of herself.

First impression of him notwithstanding, when she'd spoken with Colin two days ago in the auditorium and he'd voiced his very clever and fervent thoughts on Maslow's theory, she'd sensed something exceptional about him, something that drove away every thought of his scruffy appearance and reeled her in to his charm. He fascinated her with the inkling that there was something more to him than his outward appearance.

Something extraordinary.

His eyes. His beautiful, sea-blue eyes. When he spoke about anything, they danced with happiness and amusement. When he spoke about God, they blazed with love, fire and excitement.

She couldn't help but want to find out more about the man. She wasn't ready to pursue a relationship with anyone, but she could use all the friends she could get. And she wanted to get to know more about Colin.

It wasn't as if she were attracted to him or anything. Not *that* way. He was hardly her type. *Her* type of man was a stylish, well-dressed, aggressive overachiever who cared more about himself and his career than he did the woman he supposedly loved.

Which was exactly why she was swearing off the whole gender. One-hundred-percent cold turkey.

Except for Colin. And it appeared *he* was swearing off *her*. She glanced once again at her watch and decided she'd waited long enough.

She gathered her bag, concluding it was pointless to stay any longer. He was obviously not going to show up, and the longer she waited, the more she was going to hurt herself.

Maybe he never planned to come in the first place. And since she hadn't thought to give him her cell phone number, he wouldn't have been able to contact her if something important *had* come up, and he couldn't make it for legitimate reasons.

"Fair Holly, your carriage awaits."

Even as her heart skipped a beat at his fairy-tale teasing, she whirled around on the bench, her gaze narrowing in on the errant charmer. She was determined to give him a piece of her mind before she lost her nerve to the tune of his sweet words.

With a pointed glance at her watch, she stated the obvious. "Colin, it's 11:15."

He chuckled. "Thank you, *Ms. Big Ben,* for the update."

"Oh, and *Mr. Late* ought to be the one to talk. Should you be in kindergarten instead of college? It's apparent you can't tell the time."

To her surprise, he agreed. "I probably should be in kindergarten, at that." He pulled up the sleeve of his black Mickey Mouse sweatshirt and bared his arm to her perusal.

"Showing me your muscles?" she teased.

"Showing you my watch. See?"

"You aren't wearing a watch."

He broke into a grin, as if she'd made some great discovery or major breakthrough, with his help.

"Exactly," he confirmed.

"Exactly...what?" she asked, suspecting she really didn't want to know.

"I don't wear a watch."

"I think we've established that fact." If his goal was to get her laughing, and she thought it might be, he was succeeding admirably.

But there was still the issue of his standing her up for an hour. "We agreed that we were going to meet at 10:00 a.m. sharp, as I recall. If you weren't going to meet me here when you said you were, why did you bother to mention a specific time at all?"

"I didn't mention a specific time. You did. Besides, I'm here now. Isn't that what's important?"

"Isn't keeping your word important?" she shot back, annoyed, but she regretted her hasty words when his face colored scarlet.

He had the nerve to look angry? Indignation rose tightly within her. She pinched her mouth closed, her heart pounding rapidly in her defense. *She* was the one who'd been injured here.

"Yes, ma'am, keeping my word is very important to me," he replied gravely, his golden brows bridging low over his eyes. "I guess I should have told you up front that I—I don't live by my watch," he stammered.

His gaze met hers, then he looked away. "I expected to arrive much closer to our scheduled meeting time than I did. I do apologize for that."

She was intrigued. There was a story here he wasn't telling her. Why would a man forswear a watch, particularly when he was in college, where time was so very much of the essence?

"So tell me, Colin...how do you make it to all your classes without knowing what time it is? Since you don't wear a watch."

He shrugged, and his face pinched up so it looked almost like a cringe. "Well, I know you saw me sneak in late to your class the other day, so I guess I can't deny it. My system's not perfect."

"Oh, it's not *my* class," she corrected, heat warming her cheeks at his assumption. "I'm only a student teacher at the moment. For my doctorate, you know? There are two of us team-teaching the child psychology class this semester, under a full professor's guidance."

"Oh? I thought you were a full prof-ess-or." He slid down to sit beside her on the bench. "You certainly talk the game. Imagine my surprise when I arrive at my very first college class only to discover that my university teacher is cuter than I am."

Her face was now utterly flaming. He might not be the best-dressed man she'd ever known, but he had the silver tongue of a devil in disguise. She'd have to watch herself around his blatant flattery, or she might just wind up believing him.

"So what about your system? Do you just guess what time you're supposed to be in class?" she asked in a rush of breath, trying desperately to turn the subject away from herself.

"More or less. I do have an alarm clock. On school days I usually haul myself out of bed in time to make it to my first class."

He grinned and gave a casual shrug. "From there, it's just a matter of moving from building to building. The timing is about right for me to make it to my next class with extra to spare, and my courses at the university are all in a row, so I don't have any downtime."

"Not even for lunch?"

"Nope." He winked. "I brown-bag it. Eat in one of my classes. Not yours," he added hastily.

"For some pathetic reason I believe you," she said, shaking her head. "But that still doesn't explain why it took you so long to get here today."

He flashed her a twisted grin but kept silent.

She wasn't about to let him get away with it, even though he was silently begging her for mercy. "You know you're going to tell me, so you might as well just spit it out and be done with it."

He probed her soul with his gaze, looking as if he were about to refuse to say a word. Then, suddenly, his gaze grew clear, and he relented. "I rescued a litter of kittens."

Holly made a little squeaking sound out of the back of her throat—the best she could do for speech at the moment.

He cleared his throat. "I found them abandoned in the Dumpster at my apartment. What could I do? Just leave them there to fend for themselves?"

She couldn't help it. Her heart went soft, and no amount of coaxing could harden it up again. Colin Brockman was a hero, and what was more, he didn't even like admitting to the fact.

Unless he was just teasing her, testing her resistance to the romantic.

"You're kidding, right?" she asked, secretly hoping he wasn't.

His sea-blue eyes widened as he scrubbed his hand through his tousled blond hair. His mouth puckered in a reluctant half smile, and he shifted his gaze back to the ground. "What do you think?"

She sighed and reached for his arm, sliding her palm up to the breadth of his shoulder. Her fingers didn't miss the depth of muscle hidden beneath his cotton shirt. Colin was every bit as strong as he looked. "I think I'm a sucker for kindness. How many kittens were there? And what did you do with them?"

"One question at a time, please. There were six little kittens. Newborns. Four black, one white and one little guy, the runt of the litter, with black and white patches all over him."

Holly made a tender, choking sound in her throat and Colin lifted an amused eyebrow.

"They were stuck in a shoebox with a lid on top. Someone had taped the box shut with packing tape and tossed them into the Dumpster. I just thank God I walked by when I did."

"Poor little things," Holly cooed. "How could some terrible person abandon a litter of newborn kittens? Who would be so awful?"

"Too much trouble, I guess. Some people can't own up to their responsibilities."

"I'll say," she agreed, righteous indignation coursing through her. Poor little things. "So what did you do with them?"

"Well, I'd like to say I found nice homes for all of them. Someplace with little girls to tie bows around their necks and give them milk when they purred."

He smiled grimly. "But I did the next best thing—took the little nippers to the local Humane Society."

She could tell he was choked up about it, though he struggled not to let it show on his face or in his low voice.

"You did the right thing," she assured him, "although I know it must have been tough to let them go."

He laughed, but it was a dry, echoing sound. "You could say that." He looked around, rubbed his palms together and stood abruptly.

"So...where are we off to today?" He'd switched from melancholy to cheerful in an instant.

She stood and met his gaze, expecting to see the truth hiding under the surface; but his eyes were a clear, bright smiling blue. She couldn't keep pace with him. His erratic hairpin curves in emotion were more than she could navigate.

She took a moment to collect her thoughts. "Actually, we can walk there from here, so we won't be needing that carriage you mentioned," she said, feeling her tone might be a little too bright.

"I thought we were going to a rescue mission or something."

"That was my original plan, but as I was thinking about it, I wondered if we couldn't go a different direction for your assignment. Do something the other students might not think to do."

He smiled, and it lit up his whole face. "That sounds good to me. I'm not exactly your typical student, as if you hadn't noticed. But you know, that brings up another question.''

"Yes?"

"Why are you helping me?"

Holly froze inside. She didn't know the answer to that. "We can go the rescue mission if that's what you want to do."

"You didn't answer my question."

She pulled her book bag into her chest, using it as a shield. "No, I didn't."

His voice softened. "Why not?"

"I..." she began, and then her voice trailed off as her throat tightened. "I suppose I thought you might need help."

Colin tilted his head, silent for a moment. Then he slapped his hand against his thigh and roared with laughter. "I look that bad, do I?"

No, he didn't look bad. He looked wonderful. He'd also looked like a lost sheep that first day in class. Completely out of his element. And she'd always been drawn to the pariah. Perhaps that's why she'd responded to him the way she had.

It was as much a mystery to her as anyone.

"I didn't mean that in a bad way," she amended rapidly. "Actually, I'm just as interested in the topic as anyone."

"I hope so, considering you're a grad student," he pointed out wryly as he reached for his bag. "Is it okay for you to be helping me, Mrs. Prof?" he asked softly as he slung his bag over his shoulder.

"Ms. Prof, thank you very much. And I should think so," she answered, realizing she'd consciously set aside taking into account the ethical implications of her helping one student over the others. Would it be considered fraternizing for her to be here with Colin?

She hoped not, and for more reasons than one.

"I'm a student, too, Colin," she reaffirmed, as much to herself as to him. "I'm helping out the child psych class because my doctorate thesis is in the area of child psychology, but I'm not a full professor. So I don't see any hindrance from us exploring the first assignment, or any other, together."

"Okay," he said easily. "I'm glad."

His simple, straightforward statement took her aback. He could be frighteningly direct at times.

"What's your doctorate thesis about?" he asked as they walked, sounding, to her surprise, genuinely interested in what she had to say.

She laughed. "You don't really want to know, do you?"

He grinned back. "Why not?"

She playfully jostled his shoulder. "Because it's long and complicated. I'll tell you, if you really want me to, but not right now."

"Okay," he conceded, falling easily into step with her. "Later, then."

"Sure. Later. Right now, we'd better set our minds on *needs hierarchies.*"

"The triangle is already forming in my mind," he

teased, holding one hand to his temple as if he were conjuring the image as he spoke.

"You have some good ideas about where God fits into human need," she said on a serious vein.

"They're just thoughts," he corrected. "I've been mulling it over, but I'm not satisfied with my conclusions. It's a complex topic."

"You sound like you're trying to make it into a theological principle or doctrine of the faith," she teased. "I'd almost think you were trying to set this thing in stone."

"Maybe I am," he confessed with a ready smile. "I'm no scholar. I'm sure you've figured that out by now. But I do know that everything I learn here I'm learning for a reason. I'm also attending Stanton Seminary at the same time as the university."

Holly shook her head, shock reeling through her. As nice as he was, she just couldn't see Colin as pastor material. "You want to be a pastor?"

He laughed. "Oh, no. Not this man. A navy chaplain."

Seminary? A *navy chaplain?*

He would have done better to have left it at pastor. A navy chaplain, Holly could picture. But regret filled her. She'd been enjoying getting to know Colin. And she already knew she couldn't be a part of *this* man's navy.

Chapter Three

Colin wasn't sure what he'd said, but Holly looked as if she were ready to take a nosedive, or lose her breakfast, or maybe both. Her complexion turned white and clammy, and she was clasping her canvas bag to her chest as if it were a lifeline.

Or a shield.

He made a quick mental backtrack. He was sure he hadn't done anything inappropriate, and all he'd said was that he was training to be a navy chaplain. It was as if she'd frozen at the word *chaplain,* though moments earlier her voice had sounded teasing when she'd asked him if he was going to be a pastor.

She'd already made it clear to him she shared his faith. So what could be the problem?

He swiftly reached a hand to her to steady her, but she brushed him off with a scowl. Both literally and figuratively, he suspected.

"What did I say?" He asked the question gently, but that didn't stop her from cringing.

"Nothing." She snapped out the single word, steadfastly refusing to look at him and stepping away as if he were invading her space.

"Come on. Something I said or did made you angry." He set his backpack on the sidewalk and gestured to her with both his hands free.

She shook her head, almost vehemently. "I'm not angry."

"Then what?" he coaxed gently, adding his most winning smile for effect. Surely his immense manly charm wouldn't be lost on her, he thought sardonically.

It had always worked before.

His grin widened just as her frown narrowed. "Have you charmed your way out of *every* difficult situation you've ever found yourself facing?" she asked curtly, propping her free hand on her hip.

He scrubbed his fingers through his already-tousled hair, debating with himself how much honesty was called for in such situations. Finally he shrugged. "Mostly, yes."

She turned on her heel and faced him off with the spit and polish of a drill sergeant. "Well, it's not going to work with me, Colin Brockman."

He pulled in his smile, but knew it still tugged persistently at the corners of his mouth. Her eyes were sparkling with challenge, and he was determined to see them brimming with mirth.

With that lofty goal in mind, he lifted a hand to her cheek and slowly ran his index finger down the line of her jaw. It was extraordinary, how the rough calluses on his finger felt against the silky smoothness of her skin, as if the two were made for one another.

Callus and cream. Direct opposites, and yet the sensation of his hand on her skin was all the more breathtaking for its very contradiction.

Holly didn't speak, not even to turn him away, so he leaned into her ear and whispered, "Don't be so sure about that. I can be charming when I want to be."

Her reaction was classic, and not totally unexpected. Huffing loudly, she began marching in a direct line away from him. She didn't look back, not even to level him with a glare.

And—another point in his favor—she didn't swing her book bag at him, though he could tell the thought crossed her mind.

Laughing, Colin caught up his own bag and followed, loping to catch up with her long strides. "So where are we going?" he asked easily, as if the unusual moment between them hadn't taken place at all.

It was his way, to go on and not dwell on things. He hoped she'd follow his lead.

He'd make a point to find out later what had gotten her so ruffled. Sometimes it paid to wait until emotions had calmed before addressing matters of that nature, anyway.

Not that he was an expert. He strode to keep up with her quick pace.

They walked in silence for a moment, and then her gaze swung sharply up to him. She looked apprehensive, as if she was concerned he might be joking again, and she didn't like that prospect. He smiled to assure her he was on the up-and-up.

"The university has an extension program that works with children who have special needs," she began, putting on her teacher's voice, which Colin thought was for his benefit.

Or maybe for hers. He bit back a smile.

"It's called Marston House."

"I think I've heard of it. They take care of Down's syndrome kids and stuff, right?"

She shook her head, but her eyes were laughing. "And stuff. Oh, Colin, you're hopeless! What am I going to do with you?"

"I can't wait to find out," he quipped.

"You wish." She nudged him playfully on the arm. He grinned, happy that the easy camaraderie was back between them.

"Anyway," she continued, "I've arranged it so the children you'll be meeting today are all deaf. They take special classes to learn sign language and lip-reading, among other things. Eventually many of them learn to speak by themselves."

"Pretty impressive stuff," Colin said, uttering a low whistle. But just as he spoke, he caught the gist of her words and froze to the spot, reaching for her elbow so she wouldn't walk away without him.

"Did you say meet the kids?"

She whirled on her toes, teasing surprise registering in her eyes. "Of course I mean kids. You're in a child psychology class. And that's the assignment. Or have you managed to squirrel that away *out of sight, out of mind,* as well?" She tapped her temple with her index finger.

He grinned wryly. "Something like that. Actually, I was referring to the *meet* part of the sentence. I'm positive you didn't say anything about meeting or interacting with the children we monitor when you gave out your very specific and succinct instructions. The word I remember is *observe.*"

She looked flustered for the briefest moment, and Colin grinned. For some reason, it gave him a kick that he could do that to her.

That she could fluster him just as easily was completely irrelevant.

"Observe means to watch, view, scrutinize, monitor," he said as blandly as a walking dictionary.

"I *know* what *observe* means," she snapped, moving rapidly from flustered to annoyed. And while he enjoyed setting her off-kilter, he wasn't so sure he wanted to cross the line.

An angry woman was a volatile woman, and that he didn't need.

"It's no big deal," he said, fibbing through his teeth.

She crossed her arms and raised a dark eyebrow. "Colin Brockman, I haven't known you that long, but anyone with half an eye to see can tell you're not telling me the truth."

He slouched away from her. "How's that?" he asked defensively.

"Classic symptoms. Won't look me in the eye. Hunches away from me. Fiddles with the zipper on his jacket." She smiled, her eyes gleaming with amusement. "I'm a psychologist, remember?"

In the space it took her to say the words, he'd dropped his hand from his jacket, pulled himself to full rigid military attention, looked her straight in the eye and jammed his fingers through his hair just for good measure.

Holly chuckled, but her eyes were serious. "What's the problem, Colin?" she asked, more gently and softly than he would have expected, or maybe even thought that he deserved.

He knew he wasn't making any sense to her. He didn't make any sense to himself at times. She had every right to be annoyed with him.

Still, he wasn't one of those open, sensitive guys who bared their souls on the first date, and Holly was hitting a nerve. Thanks to God, he'd made many resolutions in his life and in his personal relationships, but he still kept his emotions tucked safely away.

Not even this pretty psychologist was going to pull his true feelings out of him, though, if anyone could do so, Holly might be the one.

"I don't like children." He knew it sounded harsh, but it was better than admitting the real truth, that he was afraid of them.

Holly made a sound from the back of her throat that was close to a snort. That was about as much nonsense as she had ever heard from a man, and she told him so.

"You don't have to meet the kids if you don't want to, but I think you may surprise yourself. From everything I know of you, I believe you'd be good for them. They could really use your attention."

Colin raised his eyebrows, and a shield dropped over his eyes. He smiled with obvious effort. "All right, then. Bring them on."

Holly wanted to laugh at his forced bravado, the gravelly sound in his voice making it sound as if he were walking the plank.

But found she couldn't laugh at him. Colin was obviously hiding something, and though she wanted to share his burden, she decided to say nothing and let this hand play out on its own.

Sometime soon, she would discover what was haunting him. What was the mystery, the hidden crisis he veiled so well behind his casual demeanor?

It might be the psychologist in her that wanted to know the truth, but Holly suspected it was the woman.

Very much the woman.

As they entered the school facility at Marston House, Holly greeted the administrator, who led them to a large playroom filled with equipment. A large, multicolored plastic jungle gym took center stage, surrounded by various-sized rubber balls, a teeter-totter and a number of gymnastics devices, including rings, parallel bars, a balance beam and a gymnast's horse.

To one side, a group of elementary-aged children sat in a circle on the floor, practicing their hand signs in an animated display.

Colin stepped so close behind Holly that she could feel his warm breath prickling on the back of her neck, even before he spoke. As if he'd done it a million times, he placed his hands on her shoulders and rubbed his thumbs gently against her sore muscles.

Her own breath caught so suddenly in her throat that she was afraid to speak, for fear he'd be able to hear the emotion in her voice and comprehend how his nearness was affecting her.

"Do you know any of that stuff?" he queried softly. For once, she heard no hint of merriment lining his voice. Awe, perhaps, and a little fear, but not the laughter that was his captivating trademark.

"Stuff?" she parroted, wishing he would step away

from her, but not finding it in herself to make the move on her own.

He wrapped his arms around her and demonstrated with his hands in front of her chin.

"This," he said, touching his index fingers together.

"And this." He touched his right middle finger to his left palm, and then reversed the action.

She was impressed. He'd been paying attention.

"And this." He wiggled his fingers in a nonsensical manner. She felt rather than heard laughter frothing to the surface.

She laughed and turned out of his grasp. "The first, I can tell you, means *to*. The second sign is *Jesus*, which is obvious, when you think about it."

"The nails in His hands."

"Right. And as far as the third sign goes, I'd have to say you need to learn how to finger spell."

"And here I thought I was so close." He wiggled his fingers again in nonsense language.

Holly ran down the finger-spelling alphabet with him, amazed at how quickly and accurately he picked up each letter sign.

"Hey, wait a minute," he broke in, midalphabet. "This is a university-run school."

Holly nodded, but didn't comment, not knowing where he was going with his point.

"Why are the children learning how to sign *Jesus?*

Isn't that a breach of separation of church and state or something?''

Holly would have bristled at the question, were his tone not so reverent and sincere.

''These kids have to learn everything they need to survive out in the world. Part of that world is faith and God and church. So the kids learn the signs they'll need to know to follow along with the praise songs and hymns, not to mention the sermon. I don't know about you, but my pastor preaches about Jesus a lot.''

Colin chuckled, remembering the cantankerous old hellfire-and-brimstone navy chaplain who'd helped him see the light. What if he hadn't been able to hear the old man's preaching? It was so easy to take God's gifts for granted.

There and then he prayed silently in gratitude for his own blessings, and resolved himself to brighten these courageous young children's hearts in some way this day.

His heart felt heavy with their burden and light with God's peace at the same time. It was a funny, choked-up kind of feeling, and Colin wasn't sure what he should make of it.

''Do they have special deaf churches?'' he asked in an attempt to cover his own discomfort.

''No.'' Holly took Colin by the elbow and nudged him toward the group of children. He offered a token resistance, but it was no more than that.

He knew it was a ploy, and he suspected she knew it, as well.

His cover was blown. He did care.

"Most of these kids go to one of the larger churches around town, one of those that offers an interpreter for the deaf. Greeley's a good town to grow up in if you're deaf. The college draws in students wanting to learn to work with the hearing-impaired, so there is no shortage of eager interpreters."

"That's good to know," Colin said, but his focus had already shifted to the children.

It was obvious the moment they got the go-ahead to break out of the group and play. Children scattered like a flock of chickens with a fox in the coop. Smiles and laughter abounded all over the place.

"It looks and sounds just like a regular playground," Colin murmured in awe and wonder. "This is absolutely incredible."

"What did you expect?" she asked softly.

He looked down at her warm, velvet-green eyes and shook his head. "I've learned not to have expectations." His voice lowered and he frowned. "Somebody always gets hurt."

She slid her palm over his forearm, intensely aware of how his muscles tightened under her touch. "'Somebody,' meaning you?" she queried gently, keenly aware of the risk she took in asking.

He shoved his hands into the front pockets of his

jeans, effectually brushing her hand away from him. "Sometimes."

It was little more than a whisper. Colin obviously didn't want to talk about it, but Holly didn't realize how much until he abruptly turned and strode away from her, taking refuge with the children he'd earlier professed to dislike.

He singled out a young boy who was tossing a rubber Four Square ball against the wall in an empty rhythm. He was all alone in his corner of the room, and he appeared not to notice when Colin approached him.

Holly cringed inwardly. Of all the children to pick, Colin had to go and choose the one least likely to respond to him. He was in trouble again, and he didn't even know it yet.

She started to follow, but her determination to save Colin from himself came to a screeching halt, as did her feet, when Colin appeared to strike up a conversation with the young boy.

It was impossible.

Well, perhaps *impossible* was too strong a word. But highly unlikely, from a large, untrained, blustering hulk of a man like Colin Brockman.

The boy was nine-year-old Jared Matthews, a mildly autistic boy counselors had as yet been unable to reach with any effectiveness. He wasn't deaf, but he often fled reality for a world of his own, somewhere deep inside his head where he could make sense of a life that flew by too fast, too strong and too loud for him.

Like many autistic children, Jared was very smart and clever, amazing others with what he could do. Music was his forte. Without any instruction whatsoever, he could play any instrument given to him. He had a natural ear for music, and played beautiful songs he made up in his mind.

But that was only when he could pull himself from his autism, and it was becoming increasingly difficult for him to do so. More and more, he retreated into a world of his own making, rather than living in the real world.

The fact that he had been shifted from foster home to foster home during his young life didn't help. He'd been all but abandoned by parents who didn't want the trouble of an autistic son, and Holly was certain it wouldn't be long before the parents made it official.

She hoped—prayed—she was wrong.

Parents didn't abandon their children, even those with disabilities. She'd been raised to believe that family took care of their own.

Her heart welled up, as it always did, for the boy and his terrible, tragic situation, especially knowing there was nothing she could do about it.

That was the worst part, knowing she could only help so many, when there were so many more in need.

Colin crouched down to the boy's level, his movements painstakingly and laboriously slow. With even

more care, he gently reached toward the boy, and
when Jared didn't protest, he tousled the boy's inky
black curls.

To Holly's great surprise, not only did Jared not
pull away from Colin's touch but, within moments,
he'd focused his gaze on the man, and was playing
against Colin in a game of Two Square.

Impossible!

Chapter Four

Holly was dumbfounded. Colin was playing Two Square with an autistic boy as though it were no big deal. As if he were an expert in the field. As if he didn't have a care in the world.

This from a man who professed a blatant dislike—or more accurately, as Holly suspected, a *fear*—of children. She didn't know what Colin had done to put Jared at ease, but in her mind, it was nothing short of a miracle, quite literally a work of God.

Surely Colin would have to realize what a special gift he'd been given. And if he didn't know, she fully intended to be the one to tell him. She suspected he'd only deny the truth, but she was compelled to confront him with the obvious.

Someone had to tell him he had a gift, or he might wander aimlessly for the rest of his life. He was a strong man with much to give the world, and if she didn't miss her guess, especially to give needy children.

All that was left was for him to figure that out for himself.

She started across the floor, her pace quick and determined. Her movement alerted Colin, whose gaze switched away from Jared to her. Their gazes met for only a moment, but it was enough for him to realize her intentions, or at least to guess at them.

It was as if she'd pushed his panic button. Alarm sparked from his sea-blue eyes, and in a moment, he was off and running.

Literally.

It was a clear attempt to avoid her, but for some reason, she didn't take it personally. She'd always had a penchant for the tousled stray—this one just happened to be a man. She'd catch up with him sooner or later.

Holly chuckled when Colin began walking hunched over like a big gorilla, touching his toes and making hooting noises. And she wasn't as surprised as she might have been when Jared followed, placing his hands on his toes and echoing the high-pitched monkey sounds.

He mimicked Colin yet again when Colin threw his arms in the air and waved them wildly, whooping like a man gone wild.

The comical little parade didn't stop when Colin

braved the balance beam, pretending to waver in the middle and making all kinds of funny faces.

And it was not only Jared aping his antics. One by one, each of the deaf children joined the line, smiling as they pretending to waver in the middle of the balance beam, just as Colin had done, making the same faces he had made.

In and out of tunnels, up and down the slides they went, one by one. Over the vaulting horse and somersaulting across the mats they flew.

Colin led and the children followed. And the merriment didn't end until the regular teacher signaled the close of the session by flickering the lights, so the children would know it was time to return to class from their play.

Colin, his face flushed, and dabbing at his sweaty temples with the edge of his shirtsleeve, looked absolutely elated.

"Did you see that?" he asked, sounding amazed and grateful, and not the least bit superficial.

"I told you, you're a natural," she teased, unable to stop herself from rubbing it in just a little bit. "Do you want to come back again sometime and play with the *children* again?"

His eyes widened, full of emotion she was certain he didn't want her to see.

"Yes." He nodded.

"No." He shook his head.

He halted abruptly, his mouth hanging open, before

he swallowed hard and jammed his fingers through his hair, sending it spiking every which direction. "I don't know, Holly. I don't really know what just happened."

His voice sounded strained, as if he were under a tremendous amount of pressure. And maybe he was.

Holly linked her hand through the crook of his arm and accompanied him out of the school. "You'll figure it out," she said gently. "You connected today."

"Do you think?" He sounded genuinely amazed, and more than a little choked up.

"Jared, the young boy you were playing with, seldom responds to contact. What you did today was a major breakthrough for him. The counselors at Marston will be thrilled."

She slid her hand down his forearm and linked her fingers with his. "I think God has given you a special gift, Colin."

He squeezed her hand and cleared his throat. "I'm humbled."

Holly hadn't expected such a reaction, and her throat closed around the unnamed emotions pounding through her chest. Colin was so strong, his navy background giving him squared shoulders and a powerful bearing; yet for the moment, she sensed a quietness in his soul, a new and tender sensitivity that only served to enhance his masculine image in her mind.

"I don't want you to take this the wrong way,"

she said slowly, her grip on him subtly tightening, "but I'm proud of you."

A slight flush tainted his tanned cheek, and one corner of his mouth tipped up in a grin. "Do you think?" he asked, his eyes gleaming.

"I think," Holly agreed, her voice scratchy with unspoken thoughts and unnamed emotions. She laughed as she pictured Colin being innocently followed by all those children. "You know what?"

"What?"

"I also think you are a veritable Pied Piper."

Colin stepped into the door of his small studio apartment. Dirty socks hung over the backs of the chairs and clothes were strewn haphazardly around, as if a tornado had blown through. Unwashed dishes were piled high in the sink, and books and papers littered the floor.

He took one look at the utter chaos he'd left in his living quarters and sighed deeply.

It was good to be home.

The last few weeks had proved incredibly busy, as professors and students alike shifted into high-learning mode. He hadn't been ready for the chaos on the high seas of academia.

Go to class.

Take good notes.

Read the textbooks.

Study for exams.

Colin barely knew what to make of it. He hadn't been in school for years, and had certainly never taken such a heavy academic load. He felt as if he were scrambling to keep up. At his best, he'd never been a model student and he didn't feel remotely close to his best at the moment.

It was the first time in his life he'd really wanted to succeed in school, but he felt as if he was not achieving the levels of accomplishment for which he was aiming.

A weekend of PT and reserve training was a welcome relief. The physical training was a terrific opportunity to stretch his idle muscles stiff from hours of cramped study, and the navy structure a good break from his self-imposed anarchy.

He'd also hoped his reserve work would give him some distance, some perspective on his thoughts, for no matter how hard he tried, or how much he studied, he couldn't seem to get Holly McCade out of his mind.

He'd seen her now and again over the weeks, passing in the halls, before and after class, always greeting one another and promising to get together for coffee, but never quite making the connection.

And he wasn't positive it was all coincidental. On a subconscious level, he thought he might be avoiding her.

Which was ridiculous. He ached to be with Holly. He thought about her every waking moment.

Yet he was obviously avoiding every opportunity to be alone with her. And it was possible she was doing the same with him.

No. He couldn't blame it on her.

He was at fault, and it was about time he acknowledged it, though he guessed that by now Holly might be blaming herself for the fact that they hadn't connected. His limited knowledge of women, mostly from his twin sister, Callie, made him believe they were prone to shoulder the blame in most circumstances, and this was probably no exception.

He only hoped he hadn't inadvertently hurt her. And he kicked himself for only now realizing that as a possibility.

He wasn't even quite sure why he was running away, except that his life was a tangled mess right now and he felt he needed to sort out the pieces before he spent any more one-on-one time with Holly.

Being with her was a roller-coaster ride in itself, without all these other things going on in his life. He was too confused to add his unquestionable attraction to Holly into the equation.

Callie was bugging him to come up to Oregon to be with her and her husband, Rhett, for Thanksgiving, but he wasn't sure he was up for the trip. Being with Callie would simply reopen old wounds about his family.

Bathed in the love of her new husband, Rhett Wheeler, Callie had succeeded in putting the past behind her, where it belonged. Colin knew what he'd find at Callie's—a traditional Thanksgiving dinner with all the fixings, followed by a jaunt to the church for a Thanksgiving praise service. God at the center, family most important and children all around.

Rhett and Callie had two children—a teenage son, Brandon, who was Rhett's from a previous marriage, but whom Callie loved as her own; and a capricious baby girl who was the apple of Rhett's eye.

Between the two of them, there was enough noise to drown out Puget Sound. And more happiness and giggles in one place than Colin thought his heart could bear right now.

He was happy for his sister, but he was envious of her, too. And he wasn't sure that now was a good time to rub his own nose in his shortcomings.

He didn't blame Callie for trying to get everyone together for the holidays. In fact, he appreciated that she always thought to include him, knowing he had no one else and nowhere to go; and no doubt realizing how much she now had, how much God had blessed her in her husband and children.

Colin unbuttoned his dirty blue shirt and twisted out of it, not caring where it dropped. He pulled on his T-shirt to stretch it out, but he didn't remove it. It might be sweat stained, but it was comfortable.

He shifted, grimacing. Neither he nor Callie had many family traditions to pass down to their children.

Oh, his mother, when she was alive, had always

prepared turkey with all the trimmings. She'd forced the festivities and brought out the best china. But his father always managed to ruin everything. Sometimes he complained about the food, but more often he complained about Colin. Colin cringed at the mere memory of his father's harsh, grating voice.

You're a complete failure, son. You disappoint me every time I turn around.

Callie should have been born the boy. At least she got good grades and stayed out of trouble.

You're nothing but trouble.

Nothing but trouble.

Colin squeezed his eyes shut and pushed the memories away, burying them in the black recesses of his mind, where they belonged. He shouldn't have gone there, even for a moment.

It did no good to dwell on the past. But it did help him make his decision.

He'd stay home for Thanksgiving and order a pizza. Callie would understand.

He scrubbed a hand over his eyes and tried to concentrate on his future. One thing he *did* know for certain—God was working through all the things that had happened in the past few weeks, including bringing Holly McCade into his life. Colin sensed that He was changing the whole course of his future, not to mention his ministry.

His Child Psych class had started out as nothing more than a requirement on his transcript, and not one he was particularly keen on completing. Now, it had suddenly become the focus of his life, in more ways than one.

Little autistic Jared Matthews was often on his mind, and always in his heart, as he figured out new and original ways he could help the boy. Though he didn't call attention to the fact, he'd visited Jared almost daily since that first time.

Sometimes, he thought he might be making a difference in the boy's life. Often, he felt there was little he could do for the lad.

Except be there. He could do that.

Because of his work with Jared, Colin had also started considering the children of military parents, those he'd be working with as a navy chaplain, those like the ones he'd grown up with.

He desperately wanted to find something he could do for them when he reenlisted. If he could reach the children...

Finally, he felt as if he had some real direction, a place to focus his energy, as he studied and struggled to become a navy chaplain. His work at the seminary and university took on new meaning, and he found it wasn't quite so difficult to pay attention to his studies as it had been before.

He was slowly unraveling one of the most complex strands of his life, and it was exhilarating.

Motivating.

And most of all *confusing*.

The most pressing question of all still loomed in his mind. It was the main reason he'd worked his body so hard this weekend, trying to sort these things out in his mind.

Where did Holly McCade fit in?

On one hand, Colin pictured her as an angel from heaven, and not just because of her beauty. She'd taken the time to help him, to rescue a poor, helpless student when he'd been floundering, even though she didn't have to do a thing.

And somehow, she'd known just what he needed.

She'd discovered his heart, and pegged him right into his future before he himself had a clue. How had she *done* that?

With an almost deliberate intent, she'd forced him into a situation beyond his experience and control. She had lined him up with a real live child, face-to-face, where he was compelled to look into the boy's eyes and confront his own fears.

And discover his destiny.

She was incredible.

She brought out the best in him, and he thought he might be a good influence on her, as well. Was it his imagination, or did she shine a little brighter when she was in his company?

Unfortunately, that was the problem.

Holly McCade was a monumental distraction. Right now and always. He didn't trust his head when he was around her. Or his heart.

Who knew if she might steal it clean away?

He unlaced his spit-polished black boots, groaning as he took them off his feet. If his hard weekend workout wasn't enough to clear his mind, he was in a whole heap of trouble.

He couldn't stop thinking about her.

It occurred to him on more than one occasion that he might want more from his relationship with Holly than mere friendship. But that was a concept so new, he hardly dared explore it.

With the singular background of a navy career out of high school and his own poor upbringing as a child, he'd never before in his life given thought to having a real, romantic relationship.

He'd dated his fair share of women, but only on a social, casual basis. He'd not taken the same woman out more than a handful of times, and even then, he never remembered feeling remotely as he did now with Holly.

Now he was toying with the concept of making a commitment to a woman. Holly deserved no less, and he wanted above all to give her everything she deserved, the world on a platter.

A real, accountable relationship. Something permanent. Grown-up, even.

It had only taken him until he was thirty years old to meet a woman extraordinary enough to prod him into acting like an adult. Go figure.

He was treading on new territory, and he hardly

knew where to begin. He struggled to compose his thoughts.

Women, in his experience, were friends. Occasionally, they'd become innocent diversions. He'd stolen more than one kiss over the years, but nothing memorable.

Shaking his head, he grunted in frustration. A kiss was one thing, but a committed relationship was something entirely different. When he looked at Holly, he heard wedding bells ringing in his ears.

Colin slammed his hand down on the table, slicing through the silence like a knife. He hadn't so much as kissed her yet, and here he was mentally standing at the altar in a tuxedo, holding matching wedding rings in his palm.

He took a deep breath and let it out, relaxed his posture and chuckled aloud.

First things first.

He had to steal a kiss.

Chapter Five

"Holly. Holly McCade. Earth to Holly. Come in, Holly."

"I'm sorry. What?" Holly asked, reluctantly pulling herself from her thoughts.

Sarah Rembrant, her friend and co-student teacher, shook her head and belted out a laugh, loud enough to cause Holly to take a fleeting look around the room to see if anyone had noticed the outburst.

Fortunately, students were only now beginning to arrive for class, milling around with the cluck and gaggle of a coop full of chickens.

"Where were you?" Sarah asked.

"What do you mean?" Holly asked, confused. "Where was I when?"

"Just now. You were a million miles away. If I didn't know better, I'd say you were somewhere in the vicinity of cloud nine. Tell me the truth now. Have you been holding out on me? Are you in love?''

''Don't be ridiculous,'' Holly snapped back, agonizingly aware of the color rushing to her cheeks even as she said the words.

Sarah's jaw dropped in astonishment. ''You *are* in love.''

Holly scowled at her friend and waved her off. ''It's about time to start class.''

Sarah nodded, but the look in her eyes assured Holly this subject wasn't closed.

It should be, Holly thought, crossing her arms about her like a shield. She wasn't in love. No one fell in love at first sight, except in the movies.

This was real life. Savvy women dated a while before they made a commitment, and even then there was generally a long engagement.

It made sense to take her time to get to know a man, to discover his true character and whether or not she would be compatible with him. Know all his quirks and his faults, not just the charm that made a woman forget her own head.

Then, perhaps, armed with all that knowledge, it would be safe to fall in love.

She wouldn't know. She'd never been remotely close to falling in love. She was no expert in matters of love, by any means. Sarah's teasing notwithstanding.

Reluctantly shifting her mind into teaching mode,

Holly let Sarah carry most of the class, and tried not to let her gaze wander too often to the blue-eyed, ruffled-haired, heart-stealing troublemaker seated in his usual seat in the back row.

Class went quickly, to Holly's surprise, and it wasn't long before the bell rang signaling the end of class. And she hadn't looked at Colin more than a handful of times.

She'd just started gathering her notes when she heard a familiar deep, teasing voice speaking to her just over her right shoulder.

"Got a minute?"

How had he managed to sneak behind her when she wasn't looking?

Holly flashed a silent distress call to Sarah, whose eyes widened noticeably at the sight of the good-looking man who cupped his hands on Holly's shoulders and turned her gently but firmly around.

"She's got all day," Sarah said, nudging Holly toward Colin, closing what little distance lay between them.

So much for friendship.

"Thanks a lot," muttered Holly under her breath, but Sarah didn't seem to notice—she was too busy smiling and crooning at Colin, acting like—well, like a woman behaved around an attractive man.

A surge of jealousy coursed through Holly, for which she was totally unprepared, quickly followed by a rush of mortification, flooding through with the force of a deep river current.

Which was ridiculous. She wasn't the jealous type. Not to mention the fact that she had nothing to be jealous about.

She had no claim on Colin. She couldn't keep him from flashing that charismatic grin to all the pretty women he met, nor would she want to. Certainly his charismatic smile would work as well on other women as it did on her, and she was hardly going to be the one to stop it. The Dodgers baseball cap he wore low on his brow did nothing to hide the inherent happiness in his smile or the joy in his eyes.

But there it was, even if she didn't want to admit it, even to herself. Holly didn't like the way Colin and Sarah connected through their gazes, as if they were sharing a private joke meant only for two.

Then the moment was over, and Colin was once again smiling at her. It was funny how he could look at her and her surroundings just melted away. He had a way about him that always made her feel as if she were the only one in the world.

Or at least the only one in the world for him.

"Well?" he queried lightly.

"Well, what?"

"You haven't answered my question yet."

Sarah cleared her throat. Loudly. "I think I better go pick up my notes off the overhead projector," she announced in an obvious attempt to leave Holly alone with Colin. Her wink in Holly's direction was an unnecessary addition to the melodrama.

But it helped nonetheless. Relief washed through Holly along with the realization that Sarah posed no threat, to whatever it was inside her that was feeling threatened.

She steadfastly refused to even *inwardly* acknowledge why it should bother her at all, never mind try to put words to her feelings. It was a free country, and Colin was too handsome a man not to be noticed by the women around him.

She took a breath, but it caught in her throat. Her relief was short-lived, and was quickly replaced by panic as she looked up at Colin's sparkling, mirthful gaze and lazy half smile.

"Your friend is nice," he commented, gesturing a nod to the retreating Sarah.

"Yes, she is," Holly agreed mildly, watching Colin's face for a reaction and relieved when there was none.

He turned his warm gaze on her and smiled his enigmatic grin, and her heart did a back flip despite her reservations. Any thoughts of threat or panic dissipated like a bad dream in the daylight. Colin's smile alone was enough to make a woman forget her own name.

"Busy Saturday?" he asked, casually pushing a stray lock of her hair away from her face.

Instinctively, a lie sprang to her lips, a defense

against the truth. She immediately set about the task of conjuring up something interesting to say she was doing. Something other than spending the weekend alone.

But before anything plausible came to mind, Colin broke in. "I hope you'll say you're free for the day. I have something I want to show you at my apartment. Something I think you'll like. A lot."

Anything she'd been about to say was immediately lost in her interminable curiosity about all things Colin. If she were the proverbial cat, she most certainly would have expired by now.

"I'm free," she reluctantly admitted. She didn't have time to regret the words, for his eyes lit up like sparklers on the Fourth of July, glittering with delight and amusement.

"I promise you won't be disappointed."

Somehow, she didn't think she would be.

"Why don't you come over in the morning and stay for lunch? I'm a lousy cook, but I'm a whiz when it comes to speed-dialing Chinese food."

"This surprise of yours will take that long?"

His half smile appeared again, along with a healthy shade of red across the top angle against the soft scruff on his cheeks. "Aw, shucks, ma'am." he said bashfully. "You caught me red-handed."

She laughed despite herself. "How's that?"

"Well, I hoped I could persuade you to stay long enough to help me brainstorm a few ideas for my big research project in your class. You gave me a great start on your course with our first excursion, and I thought maybe you could help me out again.''

She caught his gaze and held it, questioning him with her eyes. What was really behind this half serious, half flirtatious question?

What did he really want of her?

Somehow, she knew there was more behind his outwardly simple request than met the eye.

''Oh, come on,'' he pleaded, grabbing her right hand and placing it over his heart. ''You wouldn't want your favorite elderly student to fail your class now, would you?''

She chuckled. Aged he was not. ''What do you want me to bring?'' she said on a sigh. ''I make a grand tuna salad, if you're interested.''

His blue eyes sparkled like a mountain stream in the sunshine. ''Just bring your beautiful self. We'll let the lunch plans take care of themselves.''

''Colin,'' she objected, ''you are completely incorrigible.''

''I was going to say *adorable*,'' Sarah inserted as she sashayed by with a load of textbooks in her arms.

''Thanks for the compliments, ladies,'' Colin said, tipping off his baseball cap and swinging it around in a grand gesture. ''I'm going to have such a big head my cap won't fit.''

''You consider *incorrigible* a compliment?''

"You don't?" he asked, sounding genuinely surprised.

She nearly choked on her laughter. "Not in the general scheme of things."

"Oh, now, come on! Who wants everything to be the same all the time?" He punctuated the statement with a wide, confident grin that made Holly wave her hands and roll her eyes at him.

"You never know what to expect when you're with me, right?"

That, at least, was the truth.

"It's always an adventure when you're with Colin Brockman," he asserted smugly. "Always fun and games. Something new around every corner."

"You make that sound like a good thing," she muttered under her breath.

He froze in his tracks for a moment, watching her keenly and looking as if he couldn't quite figure out what he was seeing.

She wasn't surprised. She and Colin were as different as day and night in every way.

And yet there was that *adorable* thing.

Colin was that, surely, and Holly hadn't missed the fact. She had to admit she was attracted to him, but she was terrified of him, too. Jumping off cliffs without knowing if there was an ocean beneath her just wasn't her style.

Not anymore.

She gritted her teeth and closed her eyes against

the dark memories threatening to surface. Now was not the time to drudge up past mistakes.

She needed to stay with the program. Stay in control of her life and her feelings.

But with Colin, she just couldn't say no.

When he smiled, his whole face smiled. His whole *body* smiled. And when he opened his arms to her, she didn't resist. He was tall, and strong, built like a fortress, and navy tough. And he smelled wonderful—a clean, soapy scent that tickled her nostrils and made her want to inhale deeply.

She could feel the rumble of his chest on her cheek as he spoke.

"We'll stick with *incorrigible,* then," he said softly, next to her ear. "The good kind."

"If you say so," she mumbled into his shirt.

"I do," he agreed with a nod. "So hold on tight, sweet Holly, and get ready for the adventure of a lifetime."

Chapter Six

As Saturday arrived, the bright Colorado sun shone high in the sky, promising another fine fall day in the shadow of the Rocky Mountains majesty. Colin whistled under his breath as he searched for his key to his apartment door, happy, for the moment, just to be alive and breathing.

That is, at least until his gaze rested upon Holly, leaning impatiently against his front door and looking as if she had a few choice words for him. He didn't know exactly what time it was, but he guessed by the exasperated look on her face that she'd been waiting for him a good long while.

He *had* said to meet him here in the morning, he realized with a prickly brush of hindsight that left him feeling genuinely chagrined. Jumping into motion to cover his mistake, he jammed the key into the lock, stumbling over himself as he tried to express how apologetic he felt at having left her waiting.

In the end, he could only state the obvious without blathering on like a complete idiot. "I'm sorry. I know I'm late."

Holly lifted her forearm and gazed pointedly at her watch. "*Very* late."

Colin shrugged and motioned at his wrist. "I don't have a…"

"Watch," she completed for him. "Yes, I know. We've been over this before. Otherwise I would have left a long time ago. As it is…"

"I didn't mean to make you wait," he said, rubbing his palm across her shoulder, brushing back the soft, sable curl of her hair.

She chuckled. "I know you didn't. I came prepared this time." She pulled a paperback book out of her purse and waved it under his nose.

"Something for your doctorate?" he queried, lifting an amused eyebrow.

She flipped the cover to reveal the title. He recognized it to be one in a mystery series, one with a cat as the main character.

"I suppose I should be studying my psych books," she admitted with a grin. "But I thought I'd take a break today, it being Saturday and all."

"Works for me." Colin unlocked the door and gestured her in. "I'm all for taking a break whenever you can squeeze them in." He looked back at her and grinned. "Saturday. Monday. Wednesday..."

He stopped short when he surveyed his apartment, and Holly plowed right into his back, mumbling something under her breath about "brick walls."

He had more pressing matters weighing on his mind. What would she think of him when she saw his living quarters?

If anything, his front room looked *worse* than it usually did.

Was that possible?

He'd been meaning to give his present barracks a thorough scrubbing down this morning, but then an opportunity had come up that he just couldn't pass up on, and he'd gone off without giving another thought to the state of his dwelling.

And now, he was going to live to regret that easy dismissal.

Holly was practically openmouthed as she stared at his living room, arms akimbo as she confronted the slapdash, careless environment that was the true indication of his chaotic lifestyle.

Hopefully she wouldn't judge him too harshly. The mess didn't make the man, did it?

He cringed inwardly and struggled not to demonstrate his discomfort on the outside. He wanted to wiggle and squirm like the worm he was, living in a hole filled with dirt, or at least dirty laundry.

Holly turned to him, her face a mixture of emotions. "The socks strewn across the top of the furniture give the place a certain kind of ambience, don't you think?"

It was the last thing he could have expected her to say, and it threw him off for a moment. "I...uh...that is..."

"I know, I know. Your maid hasn't been here yet today." She moved to the orange patterned couch that looked—and probably was—from the seventies. With a gentle smile, she casually brushed the clutter aside, seating herself straight-backed and elegant, as if she didn't have a care in the world, and wasn't bothered at all by the disorder around her.

He recognized what that action cost her. He'd known her long enough to know she was the queen of order. If her meticulous appearance wasn't a dead giveaway, her scrupulous school notes and flawless handwriting would be enough to suggest her tendency toward, if not perfectionism, then at least chronic neatness. She was stretching herself for him, and he appreciated it more than he could express.

With a grin, he sprawled on a green armchair across from her, kicking one leg over the arm of the chair and propping one elbow on his thigh. He might not be able to voice his gratitude, but surely she'd be able to see it written on his face.

"So where were you today?" she asked, pulling her legs beneath her and leaning back against the cushion. "Or is it a state secret?"

He chuckled. "No secret. I was over visiting Jared Matthews at Marston House. I try to get by and see him every day, if I can."

Her eyebrows hit the ceiling. "Michelle Walker, the principal at Marston House, mentioned in passing that you'd been visiting Jared occasionally, but I had no idea you were growing so close to the boy."

He looked away and shrugged. How could he explain the feelings he had toward Jared?

In some way, that brave youngster represented the struggle Colin had gone through himself as a boy; and, in turn, every wretched mother's son trying to make the most of a tough situation.

He found he wanted—*needed*—to do something to make Jared's life better, to help him find a little happiness in the world. The kind of happiness Colin himself had missed as a boy.

He couldn't change his own circumstances or his past, but he would do what he could for Jared. It was the least he could do. And the most.

"Do you think you are getting through to him?" she asked softly. "Is he making any progress?"

Again, Colin shrugged. "Sometimes. Other times it's like he's completely locked away in his own mind, and all I can do is sit quietly beside him and wonder what he's thinking inside."

He crooked his elbow on his knees and gazed out the glass double doors that led to a small wooden balcony overlooking the apartment parking lot. Jared

Matthews grabbed at something in his heart. How could he express what he felt, when he wasn't even sure he could put it into words himself?

"Whenever I get through to him," he continued, "I feel like I make a genuine connection. Like the two of us have something special."

He paused and scrubbed his fingers through his hair. "Other times, I just sit and visit with him, talking about all kinds of stuff even though he doesn't respond to me. I'm not completely sure he knows I'm there."

"He knows." Holly's sweet, gentle voice soothed the ache in Colin's heart.

"Yeah," he agreed quietly, closing his eyes to hold on to the comfort. "I guess he does."

"It's too bad Jared's in such a bad situation," she remarked regretfully.

The hair on the back of Colin's neck brushed to attention. He had the distinct impression she wasn't talking about Jared's autism when she mentioned his *situation*.

He cleared his throat. "How's that?"

"You don't know?"

He shook his head.

"I would have thought Michelle or Janice at Marston House would have told you, since you're seeing Jared so regularly."

"Told me what?"

She pinched her lips together before answering, her

velvet-green eyes awash with compassion. Colin suspected that emotion might extend to him, as well as the little boy in question, and he didn't know what to make of it. He swallowed hard.

"Jared was just removed from his ninth foster home. He's having a great deal of trouble staying in a foster home setting, and foster parents just don't seem to know what to do with him."

He blew out a low whistle. "Oh, wow."

"Yeah. It's bad. He can't seem to find a good match with a family, and I think he's just miserable. The worst part is that his real parents hardly ever come see him."

"You're kidding." Colin emitted a low growl. He knew what it was like to have a father who paid no concern to him.

"I wish I was." Holly shook her head. "They've practically abandoned him to the state, though they haven't made any formal petition. I have heard they've indicated to the staff at Marston House that they can't handle a little boy with autism. Isn't that sad?"

Colin didn't answer. He was lost in his own thoughts, his mind going back to the moment in his own life when his dad ordered him to leave the house, to attend military school in another state.

Because his father couldn't handle being around *him* anymore.

"What kind of parents abandon their kids, even

when they have problems? Can you even imagine?'' she continued.

He could imagine.

He looked up at her, biting the inside of his lip until it bled in to control the emotions roiling through his belly. He was plunging into deep water here.

He hadn't told Holly the truth, or at least not the whole truth. The only ones who currently knew anything about his past relationship with his father were his twin sister, Callie, and her husband, Rhett.

And they never talked about it.

Neither did he.

But he was going to talk now. He didn't know why, but he sensed, somehow, that it was important for Holly to understand where he was coming from, why he believed the way he did about children. About families.

And that meant breaking his self-imposed code of silence.

He cleared his throat. ''When I was sixteen, I got into trouble with the law.''

He heard her sudden upsweep of breath and grinned mildly. At least he could be sure he had gotten her attention.

''I was arrested for shoplifting at a grocery store. It was on a foolish teenage dare with my twin sister, Callie, and it was only a candy bar.''

He waited for her response, but she remained silent,

staring at him with wide eyes brimming with disbelief.

He laughed. "I promise I've never done anything as remotely stupid before or since," he assured her.

Her facial color had heightened to a healthy rose, and he wondered if she regretted being here with him now. Was she going to spend the rest of her life staring at him as though he were a common criminal?

He cringed at the thought that he might have impeded on their friendship by sharing such information. Had he said the wrong thing again?

"What happened?" she whispered coarsely, clearly aware that the black moment in his story was yet to come. She sounded a little like a small child eager to hear the ending to a good story.

But at least she didn't sound judgmental. He found the courage to continue in that.

Colin ran a hand down his jaw, reluctantly remembering the moment. "My father hit the roof, and was as close as he'd ever been to hitting *me*."

Holly made a strangled noise in her throat, and he moved over to sit by her, draping his arm over the back of the couch. She leaned in to him, laying her sweet cheek on his chest as if trying to find his heartbeat.

If she *was* trying to find his heartbeat, she'd find it racing. He focused his mind on continuing his story, and found his thoughts difficult to collect.

"My dad was so angry, he threatened to send me

away to a military boarding school. I thought he was kidding. Or maybe I hoped he was just threatening me in anger, and didn't really mean what he said. But the next day, he was on the telephone, calling around to find me a boarding school. He was looking for something as far away as possible. Out of state, at least. Something in the next galaxy, I think.''

He blew out a breath. He thought he'd dealt with all his anger, but it was still difficult to look back to the trauma he'd experienced in his youth without some stirring of emotion. And he sure wasn't finding it easy to talk about, either.

"I can't believe a father would not want to be with his son," Holly said, anger tinting every word.

"Believe it," Colin snapped. "My father just wanted me to go away. In fact, I think he wished I had never been born.''

Holly made a strangled sound.

Colin grit his teeth. "When I left home, the only thing he said was that he hoped that the military could beat some sense into me."

"Well, they clearly failed," she teased softly, and Colin's gaze flew to hers. Her eyes were full of sadness and sympathy, but she was clearly trying to lighten the mood, and Colin could have kissed her for the effort.

"So true." He chuckled wryly. "I never could seem to bend myself to appreciate the military lifestyle.''

She shook her head and laughed a little too brightly. "That from a career navy man. I don't think I'll ever figure you out."

"Sounds pretty bizarre, doesn't it?"

"If I didn't know you, I'd say *yes*. But I think I understand the paradox in this case. I do want to know what happened, though," she said, once again changing the tenor of the conversation, gently nudging back toward the subject of Jared Matthews. "Having a father turn you away from home is a lot for a young man to swallow. But you turned out terrific, so you'll have to tell me how it's done."

"The word is *abandoned*. No matter how you couch it in other terms, the fact is that he abandoned me. Intentionally."

"Yes," she agreed mildly. "That's exactly what I'd call it. And I'm sorry, Colin."

Her gaze met his, warm and reassuring, and for a moment he let down his defenses, let himself feel once again the pain of rejection.

But this time, he had someone here with him. Someone to commiserate. Someone to care, to comfort him.

He squeezed his eyes closed, gratefulness washing through him as she gripped his hand, linking her fingers through his.

"I can't help being curious...." she said softly, pulling him back to the present.

He opened his eyes, gazing down at her and enjoying the novelty of the soft feelings swirling through his chest. "What?"

"How did you handle yourself when you found yourself in military school?" she asked with a smile that let him know her question wasn't entirely innocent. "Did you make yourself hard to live with? Refuse to concede? You simply don't strike me as the kind of man to give in without a good fight."

"Oh, I fought, all right," he agreed, torn between a smile and a frown. A dull ache started at the back of his neck and throbbed mercilessly into his head.

"What did you do? Act up in class and get kicked out of school? Beat up on other kids and take your anger out on them? Run away from the dorm and get chased through the woods by a pack of baying hounds?"

He blew out a breath. "In a way, I guess, I did all of those things. I certainly got in my share of fights. I tried to get kicked out, and ended up on K.P. or running the obstacle course at midnight in the pouring rain. I learned pretty quickly to keep my mouth shut and my opinions to myself."

"Keep going," Holly urged. "This story isn't over yet."

Colin snorted. "Hardly. I did my time. But my father didn't even bother to come to my graduation ceremony. My graduation." He drew his left hand into a fist, but stopped short of punching it into his right palm. "I decided right then and there I never wanted to see him again, not as long as I lived. I decided to disappear and never be seen again. Someplace my dad would never find me. Somewhere he'd never think to look.''

"So you…?"

He unclenched his fingers and ran a hand across his stubbly jaw, concentrating on the prickly feeling against his skin. "I joined the navy."

She laughed and shook her head. "I knew you were going to say that. But it still seems odd to me that a man who disliked military school so fervently would join the navy."

He reached out and pushed a stray lock of soft, sable hair from her cheek. Touching her grounded him, reminded him that he was his own man, thirty years old and not a boy. And he was sitting beside a beautiful, sensitive woman who at times appeared to understand him better than he understood himself.

He had a future to embrace.

But he knew that no matter how personally agonizing it might be, he was obligated to finish his story. Only then could Holly really understand where he was coming from, and what made him the man he had become.

"My joining the navy seems like the action of a crazy man. I know. I've thought about it a million times since that day in the recruiting office, wondering how I could ever have made that decision."

He snorted and shook his head. "All I can say is

that it made sense at the time. It might not have been rational, but I did have my reasons. The military lifestyle was familiar to me, however disagreeable it was. And I knew I could disappear quickly into the navy. My dad would never think to look for me in the military.''

He paused thoughtfully. ''Not that he would think to look for me at all.''

''What about your twin? Callie, right? Did you tell her where you were?''

''No. I never told her anything. I didn't make contact with her at all.'' He chuckled dryly. ''She was pretty angry with me when I finally got around to looking her up.''

Holly grinned wryly. ''I can imagine.''

''You probably can,'' he agreed. ''Fortunately for me, she's a kind, forgiving woman, and Rhett's a good, supportive husband. Thanks to him, I didn't have to live in the doghouse too terribly long before she welcomed me back home.''

''I'll bet that's a great relief to you.''

''It is. I really love my sister. I'm glad we could reestablish our relationship. I've always had a special bond with Callie, her being my twin and all. When we were younger we used to say we could read each other's thoughts. And I think it was pretty near true.''

Holly smiled again. ''I'm glad for you.''

''And in consolation, the navy's been good to me. I've been stationed on both coasts and in the Far East.

I've met a lot of good people, some of whom mentored me and introduced me to the love of Christ. And I have a lot to look forward to once I've reenlisted as a chaplain.''

"It worked out for you, didn't it?"

"God had it all in His capable hands," Colin stated emphatically, realizing after he said it, that what he said was true.

"He does, doesn't He?" Holly parroted softly.

"Which is what we've got to remember as we pray for poor Jared," he said, stealthily refocusing the spotlight. "I'm sure that his parents feeling the way they do about him couldn't have helped his autism."

"I think you're right about that. He sometimes retreats completely into himself, as you've no doubt seen when you work with him. He generally doesn't want to interact with anyone. Especially men."

She smiled gently and nodded in his direction. "And yet here you are, Colin. You have had the most success of anybody here in getting through to Jared, and in so little time, too."

He supposed he should feel proud, but he was humbled by the statement.

"I..." He cleared his throat and ran a hand over his mouth. "I...really care for the boy."

"Oh, Colin!" Holly launched herself at him, wrapping her arms so tightly around his neck he could barely breathe. "I knew it."

"Knew what?" he queried, his voice muffled by the arm of her sweater.

"I knew you'd realize your own potential. Your calling."

"My calling," he parroted, breaking her embrace as he stood and moved toward his bedroom door. He couldn't continue all this serious talk. He'd had enough talking and *feeling* for one day.

If he could *do* something, he'd do it. But he didn't want to talk about it.

He opened his bedroom door, and a scruffy little black-and-white ball of fur pounced into the living room, then rolled around and around, reaching for his tail.

Holly squealed in delight. "You didn't tell me you had a kitten."

"I didn't have a kitten, at least up until a few weeks ago. Remember our first date?"

Holly's heart jumped when Colin referred to their first meeting as a date, but she quickly reminded herself how unpredictable Colin was. He no doubt meant the word *date* in a generic sense.

"I remember you were late," she said.

He grinned and nodded. "Right. But do you remember *why* I was late?"

Holly's heart swelled as she recalled the circumstances surrounding his tardiness. She'd been so angry with him at the time, and yet he'd managed to win her over with his pathetic excuse.

And his boyish charm. "You were rescuing a litter of kittens, as I remember. You found them in a Dumpster or something."

"That's right."

"I'm sure I remember you saying you'd taken them to the Humane Society, so they would be adopted out to good homes."

He picked up the wiggling kitten and pulled it in next to his chest, slowly stroking over the small feline's back until he settled down and began purring contently in the big man's arms.

"I did. All except Scamp here. I just couldn't find it in my heart to give him away," he admitted in a low, husky voice.

Scamp. The name fit the rascally black-and-white-patched kitten. And maybe the moniker fit the man the cat had obviously adopted, as well.

"I think you two need each other," she remarked thoughtfully, studying the man and feline together. Scamp was still purring, and had curled into a ball, looking as if he was preparing to take a nap right there on Colin's palm.

"Don't let Scamp hear you say that. He thinks he is king of the world."

She laughed as Scamp pawed at Colin's scruffy chin. "He sure acts like he's king. And I'll bet you spoil him rotten, too, don't you?"

Colin chuckled, and his cheeks colored.

"I thought so."

"I'm not admitting to anything on the grounds it might be incriminating."

Holly reached forward, stroking the kitten on his ears. "Your very first kiddo, huh, Colin?"

"Hah!" Colin threw up his free hand, waving her off almost frantically. "That may be. But Scamp is the first and *only* kid I'm going to have in *this* family."

Chapter Seven

"What is that supposed to mean?" Holly snapped, more severely than she would have liked. She knew she sounded desperate, but he'd surprised her.

In a quick, defensive move, she swept Scamp away from Colin and cuddled him under her chin. He purred and rubbed his nose against her.

"Are you saying you don't ever want to have a cat again?"

She hoped.

He winked and shrugged. If he noticed her discomfort, he wasn't showing it. "Kittens are okay. I just don't want to have kids."

"You're joking!"

"After what I just told you about my own youth, you think I'd subject that kind of heart-wrenching agony on a child of my own?"

She wanted to point out the obvious, that it wouldn't *be* that way with a child of his own, but it was patently evident he was already finished listening to her.

Ignoring her attempt at conversation, he had dropped to his knees and was hissing at Scamp, who obliged by hissing back.

Colin's revelation amazed and stunned her. From what she'd seen and heard, he would make an excellent father. He was kind and compassionate, and full of the type of boyish charm that had Holly picturing him wrestling on the floor with a handful of small children.

Granted, right now it was more like a mangy, half-starved black-and-white kitten.

As bad as his childhood had been, Holly knew he was making the mistake of a lifetime to rule out becoming a father someday.

Why it should matter so much to *her* was beside the point.

Somehow, she decided with a strength of resolve that she didn't want to question, it had become her responsibility to make stubborn, thickheaded Colin Brockman see the error of his ways.

Children were a gift from God, not something to be feared and avoided. They were the very image of one man's love for his wife, and in that love, the image of God Himself.

Holly struggled to see Colin's viewpoint, to understand how he could feel as he did. Children were her livelihood, of course, so she was biased on the subject.

But more than that, she realized, children were her greatest dream.

Marrying Prince Charming and raising a house full of her own laughing children had been her heart's desire since she was old enough to understand what harboring such romantic notions was all about.

And those feelings hadn't faded over time. If anything, the older she got, the more she clung to her fancy.

At her age, it was probably no more than wishful thinking to believe she would—or even could—bear a houseful of children. Men weren't exactly clamoring to play the role of hero and father.

Or more accurately, not the right kind of man.

She peered down at Colin, who was lying on his back with the cat perched on his chest. They were both meowing at the tops of their lungs, and Holly couldn't quite decide who was outhowling whom.

Colin could be her Prince Charming, she realized with a start. If he combed his hair, tied his shoes and stopped slouching, it was possible she could picture him galloping into her heart on a white steed, with a shiny coat of armor dazzling brightly in the sunlight.

She caught her breath and held it, nibbling softly on her bottom lip. Maybe *that* was why she cared so much what he thought.

It was an unsettling notion.

"Do you want to work on your term paper?" she asked briskly, standing. Her head was reeling, and she scrambled to anchor herself back in reality. "That is why you asked me over here, isn't it? To brainstorm topics for your paper?"

He rolled over onto his knees. "I already have a topic."

"But I thought…"

He rose to his feet and grinned. "Okay, you caught me red-handed. I'll admit it—I invited you over here on false pretenses."

"To meet the cat?"

He slid a surprised look at Scamp. "What? Oh. Well, partially, I guess. Mostly I just wanted to spend some time with you."

Her heart picked up pace, sending little, tickling flutters down her neck. "I'm honored. I think. I enjoy spending time with you, too."

She narrowed her gaze on him, giving him her best *severe teacher* look. "Are you really that far along on your term paper?"

He chuckled and ran a hand across his scalp, making random points of his thick white-blond hair stand at attention. "I didn't say that. I said I had a topic. It's not the same thing."

She wasn't the least surprised. "Well, I'm glad to hear you've done that much on your paper, anyway. I'm sure it's better than some students have done, though as your teacher, I would highly suggest you motivate yourself in the near future.''

He chuckled.

''Care to share?''

He sat up and crooked his arm around one knee. His sea-blue eyes sparkled with excitement. ''I thought you'd never ask, Teach.''

She sat down Indian-style before him. ''Please, Colin. Professor lectures are all over for the day. I promise. I'm here as your friend.''

He smiled slyly and ran the back of his index finger down her cheek and across her chin. ''Are you?''

She had no idea what he meant by that comment, but her throat went dry and she found she couldn't swallow. ''I... Just call me a casual observer, then. I know you've put a lot of effort into this class, and I suspect you've come up with an interesting theme for your class project. I can't wait to hear it.''

''A casual observer, huh?'' He chuckled. ''I'll just bet you are.''

She frowned. ''What's that supposed to mean?''

''Oh nothing.'' His smile told her just how far from *nothing* he meant.

''Colin, you have five seconds to...'' she threatened with a smile.

''Okay. Okay.'' He pulled some papers from under the scratched and chipped oak coffee table that looked as if it might have come from a secondhand store, or maybe a garage sale. "My notes are right here. Some-where."

"So there's a method to your madness," she teased with a giggle. "And here I thought you were living in complete, unsystematic chaos."

"I can find what I'm looking for. Most of the time." He shuffled the papers and cleared his throat. "See? Here it is."

"Please proceed." She slipped softly into an arm-chair and leaned forward, wrapping her arms around her knees. "I'm all ears."

"My goal in completing this class is to create a program I can implement when I return to the navy as a chaplain. As you know, I've been drawn to the plight of children recently."

He paused and grinned at her. "Anyway, I began to think about the military kids I've run across while in the navy. I'm not a military kid myself, but I think there's a lot of need within the system as it stands today. These children move around a lot as their par-ents are reassigned to various duty stations. And if Mom or Dad is called in for active duty, the child may not see them at all for a long period of time."

"Wow. I'm impressed."

He grinned and winked at her. "And all this bril-liant deep thinking is a direct result of your fabulous teaching."

Holly smiled, aware he was teasing her, but flat-tering her nonetheless. "I'm glad to hear my lessons are reaching someone's ears. Sometimes when I'm teaching I think I'm speaking into empty space. That enormous vault of an auditorium echoes back at me like I'm in the Grand Canyon. *Alone.*''

"I've been listening," he said softly, rolling to his stomach and tucking his chin into his hands. "Before I started listening to you, I hadn't ever really thought about the needs of children. I certainly didn't consider the kids much when I was working as an RPS in the navy. Of course, Religious Program Specialists get more of the paperwork and less of the interaction than a regular navy chaplain does."

"You do realize that there are outside, auxiliary operations targeting Christians in the military that have programs available for military kids and teens," Holly interjected, thinking of her own experience as a marine drill sergeant's daughter.

She knew the programs well. She was a product of them. Or was that a by-product?

Not that the programs themselves were bad. They just hadn't reached and helped a teenaged Holly when she'd been calling for help.

"So I don't need to create something—is that what you're telling me? King Solomon's *nothing new under the sun* and all that business?" His voice was rough. He sounded frustrated.

"No, no," she protested immediately, causing him to grin at her in relief. "As much as these programs do, they don't reach the kids one-on-one, on a personal level where it really makes a difference. That's what you're talking about, isn't it?"

His blue eyes sparkled. "Exactly. I knew you'd understand where I was going with this."

"In that case, you'll be pleased to know the ball field is wide-open to your unique ideas. And to your enthusiasm."

He gave a low whistle. "It seems like a pretty wide ball field. I don't have a clue where to begin."

"Have you done any research on programs used in the past? Made a study contrasting their goals and effectiveness?"

"No, but I suspect there aren't many programs that would match the organization I've concocted. I can call one of the chaplains I worked with in the navy and ask him for help."

"Excellent start. You don't want to assume anything without doing your research, or you'll inadvertently duplicate something that's already been done."

His brows creased low over his eyes. "Good point, well-taken."

She smiled, glad to be able to use her years of training to help a friend. "You'll want to cross-examine the information you get from the navy with data you get from the other branches of service."

He glazed her with a sugary sweet look that melted her insides and contrarily put her on the defensive in a single glance.

"What?" She leaned forward and narrowed her eyes on him.

"What, what?" he asked, his voice and features dripping with feigned innocence.

"You know *what*. That look you just flashed me. What do you want?"

He looked away and pretended to brush a speck of lint from the shoulder of his white T-shirt. "It's nothing, really."

"If it's nothing, why aren't you telling me what you want?"

"I wouldn't ask, except that it will save me a bundle of time, and you know how you've been getting on me to make better use of my time."

She chuckled. "I just want you to be *aware* of time, Colin. I don't care how you use it."

"Yes, but if you talked to your father about the marines for me—"

"Hold it right there, buster." She stood with alacrity as she cut him off. "I'm out of here."

Her heart was pounding so glaringly in her head she could hardly hear or see, and there was a funny ringing sound in her ears.

All in all, she felt like she might pass out.

Or be sick. Either way, she wanted to be out of Colin's apartment when it happened.

"You'll excuse me, please. I've got to go." Dizziness engulfed her, and she reached for the back of the couch and struggled for a breath.

Colin was on his feet in an instant, his hands on her shoulders in a strong but gentle grip Holly doubted she could break.

"Hold on a second," he said, his voice as soft and low as the purr of his cat. "What did I say?"

"Nothing. I just have to go."

"Holly, I know you better than that. I know I've said something to upset you, and I want you to tell me what it is."

Holly unclenched her teeth long enough to answer him. "I have not, nor will I ever, go to my father for help or advice. Not ever. If you want to talk to him, feel free to accompany me home for Thanksgiving and ask him yourself."

Colin didn't know which portion of her comments to address first. "Is that an invitation?" he asked, surprised.

Her eyes widened. How had she gone from beelining her way out of Colin's apartment to inviting him home for Thanksgiving dinner?

"Yes, I suppose it is," she agreed reluctantly. In for a penny... "I know my mom would love to have you come up to the lodge with me. Just give me a heads-up so I can tell her to set an extra place."

"Heads-up," he answered immediately, and then paused, dropping his hands from her shoulders as he took a step back. He had to wonder, now that he'd already committed himself, just what he was getting himself into.

He'd accepted this invitation from Holly without a second's thought between his mind and his mouth. And yet his original, carefully thought out plans included a day of prayerful solitude on Thanksgiving, knowing that right now he had nothing to give anyone, not even his family.

Nothing emotional, anyway.

He'd even turned down the opportunity to share the holiday with his beloved sister, Callie, not to mention the prospect of spending time with his nephew, Brandon, and his new niece, Abigail.

Why did Holly's request feel so very different to his mind and heart?

Holly.

It was definitely Holly.

Holly was watching the interplay of emotions on his face and narrowed her eyes on him when his gaze connected with hers. *For once,* her expression told him, *I caught you off guard.*

If only she knew.

His unruffled, nonplussed, ride-the-wind-and-see-where-it-will-take-you attitude couldn't hold a candle to spending a day in the presence of sweet, spectacular, solidly dependable Holly McCade.

"I'll let my mom know you'll be coming," she said. "But there are conditions, Colin."

"Be on time and wear a tie?" he quipped, trying to coax a chuckle from her.

She looked all too serious as she stared back at

him. "You can start with that. My father's a stickler for those kinds of details. But it's actually my father to whom I was referring."

Colin pictured his own very intimidating version of Holly's Marine Corps drill sergeant father in his head and wondered if going to her parents for Thanksgiving was such a good idea after all.

"Should I salute?"

"Colin!"

"Sorry." He did his best to look ashamed, which earned him a reluctant chuckle. He followed with a feigned salute that Holly slapped away.

"Believe me, you'll feel like saluting when you meet my father. *I* feel like saluting him, and I've never been in the military."

He took a loud, sweeping breath and reached for Holly. She stood stiff for a moment, then allowed him to fold her into his arms.

She was very serious about her relationship with her father, and she didn't have to speak it aloud for him to see the tension she was feeling. He was obviously not the only one who had issues with a father. He stroked her hair and murmured soothingly.

He closed his eyes against the sudden longing in his head and heart to protect Holly from whatever it was her father had done to cause her such anxiety.

He'd long since given up the killer instinct that used to rise in him at the mention of the word *father,* but he was still inclined to distrust the title. He'd learned, living through the school of hard knocks, that not every father deliberately set out to hurt his child, but most managed to do a bang-up job in the end, intentionally or not.

Hence the reason he was so disinclined to have children of his own. He didn't want to hurt his own offspring, his own precious gifts of God, intentionally or otherwise.

He had enough to do just comforting damsels in distress over their own father's conduct.

With a shaky laugh, Holly sniffed and stepped back out of his arms. "I'm getting you all wet."

He hadn't known she'd been crying. She was still visibly shaken. Her fingers held a tremor as they wiped a few tears from those velvet-green eyes.

"That's okay. I'm a navy man, remember? We're used to water."

She chuckled again, this time sounding a little stronger and more sure of herself.

"You'd better hit me with those conditions while I'm still agreeable to a coat and tie," he teased in an attempt to distract her from her tears.

"It's nothing, really." She paused and took a deep breath. "Just this. Whatever you have in mind to do, or to ask my father, feel free to do it. I'm sure he'll be very helpful."

She looked over his shoulder and her velvet eyes misted once again. "Just do me a favor and leave me out of it."

Chapter Eight

Holly looked so miserable, so withdrawn, that Colin did the only thing he could think of.

He kissed her.

On hindsight, he realized it was probably not going to be the best idea he'd ever come up with, but at the moment, all he could think of was the softness of her lips, her cheeks, her hair.

Holly stiffened for a moment when his lips first brushed across hers, but she quickly melted into his embrace. With a contented sigh, she wrapped her arms tightly around his neck and pulled his face down to deepen the kiss.

Colin chuckled over her mouth. Perhaps she felt something for him after all. It was enough to make him want to shout for joy, except that he was too busy kissing her to shout.

The sensation of cradling Holly within the circle of his arms was wonderful. Everything *about* Holly was wonderful. But when he tried to express those feelings in his kiss, she backed away.

"What?" he groaned, trying to pull her back into his embrace. She resisted, turning out of his reach and wrapping her arms about herself in a manner that brooked no argument.

"Colin, what is this all about?"

She was back to her old self, serious, rigid spine and stiff shoulders. He wanted to reach out to her, to make things all right again.

He wanted to kiss her again and have her return that sentiment; but he knew from the look on her face it was a lost cause.

"I don't know what you mean," he denied, his voice low and husky. He tried to make eye contact, but she shifted her gaze away.

"We've been friends for a while, Colin, but there was no cause to kiss me."

He shook his head, disagreeing fervently. "I had a million reasons for kissing you, Holly."

"Oh, I wish you didn't." She slumped down on the couch. "This never should have happened."

Colin's mind was reeling. "I'm confused. I like you. And I think you like me. We kissed each other as a token of affection for each other. Where is the problem in that? What? You don't like me?"

She scrubbed a hand down her face, as if to wipe

off the assortment of emotions she displayed there. "I don't want to get into it. I don't even know where to begin addressing the issues that kissing you raises."

She shook her head and waved him off, as if that was that. "I'm not comfortable. Can we just leave it at that?"

But he didn't want to leave it at that. She made kissing sound like some kind of legal issue, or at least a topic for a self-help book.

He merely wanted to know what was wrong. He wanted to fix the problem.

Now.

With effort, he reined in his tender curiosity and crouched before her. Infinitely careful with his touch, he reached forward, suspending his motion until she consented with her gaze. Then slowly, his breath suspended in the moment, he lightly skimmed the palm of his hand down her upper arm.

"Understand one thing about me," he said, his voice low and earnest. "I like you. I consider you my friend. A very, very *good* friend. And I would never, ever hurt a friend."

She attempted a shaky smile, but he could feel her quivering.

"I'm sorry I'm acting like a goose," she said with a wobbly laugh. "Maybe someday I'll be able to explain why I'm acting this way." She looked away, and her eyes became glazed. "But not today."

"Not today," he repeated, half to himself, and half to her.

It didn't make sense. But then, she was a woman. Men and women weren't supposed to be from the same planets, were they? He held her close. "Please don't apologize to me." He crooked a finger and tipped her chin up until her reluctant gaze met his. "You have the right to your feelings."

She pinched her lips. "I don't know about that. But I appreciate your understanding."

Understanding might be overstating it, but there must be some label for the feelings he was experiencing right now. He grinned and tapped her on the nose. "You've got it."

He might not comprehend, but he could be supportive, even if he couldn't shake the feeling that Holly thought they'd—*he'd*—done something wrong.

He summed up his feelings. "We kissed, and it was fun. End of subject."

He stood and pulled Holly to her feet. His mind was still spinning, and his muscles needed something physical to do to lighten the mood and make Holly feel better.

"Now, why don't we go down to the park and see if we can have even more fun?" he suggested with a wink. "It'll take my mind off the pressure of finishing my project for your class."

He took her hand and guided her to the door. "And if you're *really* nice, I might even be persuaded to push you on the swing."

The phone was ringing as Holly entered her apartment. Holly threw her keys down on the table by the door and raced for the telephone.

"Why didn't you tell me?" Sarah demanded as soon as Holly picked up the receiver. "It's not fair for you to keep such a hunk a secret."

Holly's heart raced, and she labored to take in a breath. "I don't know what you mean."

Sarah barked out a laugh. "Oh, right. I'm sure you don't have a clue. As if plucking the best-looking student from the classroom and claiming him for yourself is your usual style."

"I did no such thing!" answered Holly indignantly. "And you know it."

Again, Sarah laughed. "Of course, silly. *I* don't care if you date a student."

"I'm not dating him. And there's nothing in the student teacher's handbook that prohibits my seeing someone in the class."

"Exactly," Sarah agreed easily. "So tell me all about him. I already know where you met. What else is there to tell? What? Where? And when?"

Holly cringed, knowing Sarah couldn't see her. "I'd rather not."

"What's wrong? You sound shaken up."

"I am. Something happened today with Colin that

I—well, I just think I'd be better off to find out a way to avoid him from now on.''

''Did he hurt you?'' Sarah, her voice defensive, sounded all ready to lay in to Colin, and Holly chuckled despite herself.

''No, of course not. Colin wouldn't hurt me. At least, not on purpose,'' she clarified quickly.

''Meaning?''

''I just want to back off. Things between the two of us are getting a little too complicated for me.'' She paused, easily conjuring up the handsome blond sailor. If she expelled her breath on a sigh, it wasn't on purpose.

At least that's what she told herself.

''So he's not a nutcase or anything.''

''Oh, no.'' It was amazing, how quickly she rose to his defense. ''Colin is a gentleman in every sense of the word. He's smart. And funny. And I don't have to tell you how handsome he is. I just can't be around him right now. And I can't explain it.''

She swept in a breath and darted a furtive glance around the room, searching for something comforting on which to settle her gaze.

But her pristine apartment offered little in the way of consolation. She snatched a pillow from the couch and pulled it close to her chest. ''That sounds crazy, doesn't it?''

''You said it, not me. Is he pushing for a commitment and you're not ready for it?''

Holly laughed shakily. "Oh, no. Nothing like that. But I do think he's pushing our relationship toward the next level, something more serious than a casual friendship."

"And?"

Holly clutched the telephone. "Sarah, you are one of the few people who really know me. You *know* why I can't be with Colin."

"I know why you're *afraid* to be with him," Sarah inserted. "Because of your past. But if Colin is half the man you say he is, he'll understand, Holly. You have to be honest with him. Talk to the man. You aren't the only one in the world who has ever done anything in their past they've been ashamed of, you know."

Holly felt her cheeks flushing with warmth. "I don't *want* him to understand, Sarah. I'll die of humiliation if he ever finds out the truth about me. I don't think I could handle that. I want to go back to the way things were before he entered my life."

"You can't do that."

"I know that. But I made a mistake in pursuing a friendship with him. He's just not the kind of man a woman can be friends with."

"Honey, I could have told you that with one look at the man." Sarah laughed. "But I don't mean to downplay how you're feeling. He wants more, and so do you. And it scares you to death."

"That's precisely the point, Sarah. And that's why

you've got to promise me you'll help me steer clear of Colin Brockman, and all the trouble he brings."

"Holly, I don't think—"

Holly cut her off. "Promise. You have to. With your help, I'll be able to put that blond-haired scalawag out of my mind once and for all."

"I promise…" Sarah said. Then she finished her sentence under her breath. "Not to tell you *I told you so* when this all falls apart."

The more Colin thought about his encounter with Holly, the more perplexed he became.

Sure, he'd kissed her without warning her first, but he was positive she'd been receptive to his affection, at least at the moment their lips had first touched.

So what had happened to turn her away from him?

He'd asked himself that question a million times, and each time he'd come up blank. He'd prayed over and over for discernment, for a tiny glimpse into heaven, or at the very least into the complex and bewildering mind of a woman.

No sign, wonder or great revelation came on any front, not that he really expected it. Bright lights were his style, not God's. And Colin was too restless to be motionless enough to hear the still, small voice that might really do him some good.

Worst of all, Holly was obviously avoiding him at all costs. It had been two whole weeks, and he hadn't seen her once.

No. That wasn't completely accurate.

He'd *seen* her, all right. But he couldn't get close to her, no matter how hard he tried. Every day in class, he watched her speaking, teaching a subject that lit her internal fire. He enjoyed the sight of her thick, sable hair swishing in waves across her back, and pictured those velvet-green eyes he'd come to know so well gleaming with brilliance, though he couldn't see them clearly from the shadows of the room where he always sat.

With every breath, he longed to speak to Holly, and his arms ached to hold her, to assure her nothing was wrong between them.

Nothing was wrong.

He remembered back to the first time he'd seen her. *Ms. Gorgeous Legs,* he'd called her.

She was that, all right. The memory brought a smile to his lips.

But there was so much more to Holly McCade than her pretty face and fine figure, that he couldn't begin to name them all. And there was so much more Colin wanted to learn about her.

It was an insatiable yearning, to know everything about her a man could learn. He knew this much— he connected with her on a level that had made her his closest friend, while paradoxically becoming the greatest mystery of his life.

Holly was kind and sensitive, with a sense of humor that matched his own—except for those few times he couldn't figure out. She was strong in a feminine sort of way. She knew where she belonged, and where she was going.

But she was hiding something. Some kind of secret that was keeping them apart. That was the only reasonable explanation he could fathom.

He'd glimpsed her in a hallway once and had started to approach her, but as soon as she'd seen him—and she *had* seen him—she'd turned and fled in the other direction like she had fire at her heels.

He had no doubt she was running away from him, that *he* was the proverbial fire nipping at her heels. The only question was, *why?*

What exactly had he done to strike the match?

Colin wasn't the type of man to sit back when there was a challenge to be met, and he wasn't about to let Holly run out of his life without a fight. She was the closest friend he'd ever had, except for his sister, and since Callie was related by blood, he could hardly count her.

He was going to get Holly back into his life. No argument about it.

Like the military man he was, Colin planned his strategy carefully. He would begin with Holly's friend Sarah, who had been so bubbly and flirtatious before, and had practically shoved Holly in his direction with her encouragement. Sarah now stood as staid and stoic as the walls of Jericho around Holly, acting like a fortress between her bewildered friend and Colin.

When he approached Sarah about Holly's noticeable absences in class, and the way she tactfully avoided him whenever she *was* there, Sarah cheerfully chatted around the issue. When he pressed her, she stoned up.

The walls of Jericho.

Clearly, Sarah didn't know how *that* particular story ended.

If he couldn't go to the source, he would find out through other means what was happening with Holly. Colin waited for the right moment, after class when Sarah was busy cleaning up. Sarah wouldn't run as far and as fast as her friend and colleague Holly. He could feel it in his gut.

When he advanced, it was a full-scale attack. He even sent a couple of figurative spies, in the form of jocks that sat near him in psych class whom he'd made acquaintances with, to spy out the land. They kept Sarah occupied while the classroom exited, luring her off to the side where she would be more vulnerable.

He waited in the shadows until the trumpet was sounded.

Then he charged.

Sarah saw him coming, rapidly interpreting the determined expression on his face, if her flare of panic was any indication. She scurried for her notes and books, but put them down again when she realized there was no immediate means of escape.

Where was there to run? Colin would only follow, and probably cause a scene.

Colin squared his shoulders. He was taking no prisoners. No matter what he had to do.

"I don't even know what I said," he declared boldly, taking a calculated risk that Sarah knew the whole story and would not mistake his meaning.

There was an awkward moment where the air crackled with electrical silence. She narrowed her gaze sharply upon him.

Then, all at once, the walls of Jericho cracked, and started to crumble.

With a vengeance.

"Said? What you *said?* It's what you *did,* you dumb, overgrown sailor."

Her insults didn't bother him, but her accusation cut to the quick.

He'd never knowingly hurt Holly. And Sarah of all people should know that. Was it only two weeks earlier that she'd been pushing the two of them together?

Women.

"What I did," he repeated, trying to keep the frustration he was feeling out of his voice. "And that would be *what,* exactly?"

"If you don't know, I'm not going to tell you. You'll have to take that up with Holly."

"In a second," Colin barked back, seething with annoyance. Was it just with him, or did women al-

ways talk and not say what they meant? "Except, as
you well know, Holly isn't speaking to me."

Sarah shrugged, and Colin thought he saw just a
hint of concession in her eyes. "I did tell her she
ought to talk to you."

The walls continued to crumble. He grinned. This
was one battle he was determined to win.

"I'd never hurt Holly. Sarah, if you listen to one
thing from me today, this is it. You've got to believe
that."

She pinned him with a fierce, protective glare that
spoke louder than words. He already *had* hurt Holly.

"Maybe not intentionally."

He scrubbed a hand through his hair. "Look, I'm
trying to fix the problem, whatever it is. Whatever I
have to do, I'll do it. If she'd just tell me what's
wrong, I'd have a lot better shot at making it better."

He shook his head fervently, his determination to
make things right with Holly renewing with every
breath he took. He *would* make this work. "At least
I'm *trying* to work things out with her, which is more
than you can say Holly is doing right now."

Sarah nodded. "I'll admit, that's commendable."
It sounded like half truth, half cynicism. She continued to eye him closely, taking his measure.

She was a good friend to Holly, Colin realized, but
while he appreciated her loyalty, he also wished he
could cut a break with her here. Anything would be
better than what he was feeling right now.

It was now or never to blow the ram's horn and shatter any remaining bricks. He cleared his throat and flashed her his best pleading gaze. "Sarah. Please. Give me a break. Help me out."

She narrowed her eyes on him. "I'd like to do that, Colin, but I'm not sure I can. I have a division of interests here."

"No you don't," he replied immediately. "Sarah, we're all on the same side here. You, me and Holly. We're striving toward the same goal. You've got to see that we are."

He pinched his lips together in a straight, determined line. He wasn't going to stoop to yelling at Sarah, but he figured he wasn't beyond a little begging. "Where is Holly now?"

She wavered for a moment before answering, her eyes flickering with uncertainty. "She's back in the psychology office. Doing research, if I'm not mistaken."

"Good."

"I'm sure she doesn't wish to be disturbed."

He waved her off with a shake of his head. "Take me there." It was more of a command than a request.

Sarah flipped her long hair to one side and perched her hands upon her hips. "And then what?"

Colin shrugged. "I guess we'll figure that out when we get there."

"Got a minute?" Colin peered suddenly around the side of the office door and flashed Holly a toothy Cheshire cat grin.

Holly put a hand to her chest to still her pounding heart. He'd startled her, popping in unannounced as he had; but if she were honest, that wasn't the only reason her heart was beating so rapidly.

It was the man himself. And she had no desire whatsoever to speak with him.

He knew it, and she knew it. He was purposefully backing her into a corner, and she mentally scrambled for the best way to react to his unwelcome presence.

"For you, anytime," she said, then wondering how her lips could so easily form such a falsehood. She tried to smile, and knew it looked more like a grimace, but Colin didn't appear to notice. Or if he did, he was resolutely ignoring her discomfort.

He swirled into the office like a whirlwind, pulled up a wooden, straight-backed chair, turned it backward and straddled it, leaning forward on his arms.

"So what are you up to?"

Obviously not what was really on his mind. Not even a particularly good opening line, from friends who hadn't seen each other in a while.

Holly steepled her fingers and leaned back in her seat, a big, black leather office chair that creaked when it moved. "What do you really want?"

Colin raised both his eyebrows. "You know me so well."

"Ha-ha."

"That wasn't a joke."

Holly groaned. "Everything's a joke with you, Colin. This much I know."

"You've got it all wrong," he protested.

"Do I? There is no ulterior motive for your visit today? Nothing you hoped to accomplish?"

He colored. "Well, there is that matter of Thanksgiving dinner."

"See? I told you so," she crowed, delighted at the opportunity to see Colin squirm a little bit.

"Did anyone ever tell you," he replied mildly, leaning his chin on his arms, "that it's not polite to gloat when someone's begging?"

Holly's breath caught in her throat. "You're begging?"

His clear, sea-blue gaze caught hers and held. "Do I need to be?"

She looked away. "No," she said around the catch in her throat. "I guess not."

He smiled so gently, and so completely without gall, that she instantly forgave him everything. Even stealing a kiss.

"Are you sure?" he continued, standing to his feet and yanking his chair out of the way so that the legs scratched against the tile floor. "Because I can get down on my knees right now."

Holly held both of her hands in the air, mortified. "Please don't."

He didn't. Instead, he held his hands out to her,

pulling her out of her chair until she was standing face-to-face with him, a little closer than she would have liked, but not so close as to make her back off.

"Am I re-invited for Thanksgiving dinner?" he asked in a teasing tone.

"To my knowledge, you were never uninvited," she reminded him.

"Not technically, maybe."

"Not at all."

"We're going to have to talk, you know." His words were soft, but their meaning was unmistakable. He wanted to know why a kiss could send her off the deep end.

"Do we have to talk now?"

He chuckled. "No. Just sometime."

"Sometime, then." She'd put *that* moment off for as long as possible. Now that she was in Colin's presence again, she remembered how much she liked being around him, and she wasn't quite ready to give that up.

Which she'd have to do when he found out the truth about her. He wouldn't want to be around the kind of woman she was.

"Sometime it is."

"You really want to come?" she queried softly, squeezing his fingers.

"I really do." His gaze told her how much. "I need to speak with your father, remember?"

She did remember. And she thought she should feel

insulted, for him to remind her of that. Maybe with another man, she would be.

But with Colin, she somehow knew that while he did need to speak with her father about the marines, he was really coming along to spend the weekend with her. And for now, that was all she needed to know.

Chapter Nine

One look into Colin's sea-blue eyes and Holly's common sense must have floated away. That was the only possible explanation.

And now, on Thanksgiving Day, she had to pay for her moment of weakness.

Holly straightened her jacket and slid a glance sideways at the handsome man standing beside her on her parents' front porch.

He looked straight ahead, his bearing tall and strong. He didn't appear to be looking in her direction, but just the same, as she turned her glance away from him, he reached out and grabbed for her hand, giving it a reassuring squeeze.

She smiled softly. She didn't know whether the reassurance in his grip was more for her benefit, or for his.

It was the first time she'd ever seen Colin look nervous. She thought, given the circumstances, that she might be basking in the pleasure of watching him sweat, but she was more taken in by the moment's witness of sheer humanity.

He wasn't always one hundred percent in control, after all. The knowledge made her like him even more.

Holly was a bit amused by his looks. His jeans and sweater looked as if they might have been ironed. It looked as if he'd bought a new pair of running shoes for the occasion, for the supple white leather wasn't marred by a single scuff.

He'd even combed his hair into a semblance of military precision. Not a single strand of his white-blond hair was out of place, no doubt thanks to a good slathering of gel.

She looked up at him and smiled. She wasn't at all sure she wanted him here with her today, but there was no sense in making him suffer any more than was absolutely necessary. Not that there was any doubt on that point.

He *would* suffer.

Her father would see to that, however shrewdly he crafted ways to turn the screws on Colin. It was going to be an agonizing weekend for everyone concerned, and for her most of all.

Holly made up her mind at once not to be the cause of any of Colin's difficulties. At least not today.

She closed her eyes and sent a silent and uncomfortably overdue prayer of forgiveness heavenward. It wasn't Colin's fault she had a sordid past she was struggling to keep hidden, especially when she was the one who hadn't been up-front with him in the first place. Maybe if she had been...

Stealing a kiss was not a crime.

She might even have enjoyed it, were circumstances different.

But they weren't.

She shifted uneasily. Her parents were taking an inordinate amount of time answering the door. On purpose. To keep them squirming.

Holly knew she'd eventually have to talk to Colin, and tell him the truth. Even if they never took their relationship beyond the friendship they had now, he deserved to know.

But knowing would change everything. And she would put that moment off for as long as she could. She had already waited too long to bare her soul to him, at least with any hope of his understanding. He would want to know why she hadn't been up-front with him.

And to be honest, she didn't know the answer to that question anymore. She wished she *had*.

She wasn't going to kid herself with anything but the truth. He was going to turn around and walk right out of her life when he found out how she'd spent her teenage years, what kind of person she'd been back then.

A shiver ran through her. There wouldn't be any more stolen kisses between them to worry about.

Which was all the more reason to enjoy whatever time she had left with him. She squared her shoulders. She had a lot of memories to make, something she could treasure later.

After.

She glanced sideways to see if Colin was feeling half as impatient with the wait as she was. He wasn't his usual talkative self, if that was any indication.

But when he met her gaze, all her doubts disappeared. The smile Colin gave her was anything but apprehensive, edgy or even impatient, for that matter. It was his usual careless, confident grin, and it immediately made her feel better inside.

Funny how he could reassure her even when he wasn't trying.

Her father swung the door open, and she knew in an instant he'd been making them wait on purpose.

Anger flared in her chest, but Colin squeezed her hand again, as if he knew what she was feeling, and her resolve to make the best of things strengthened. She wasn't going to let her father get the best of her. Not now that Colin was here with her.

"Dad, this is Colin Brockman, the man I told you about."

Holly's father, Ian, his hair cut in a characteristic

military crew, and his T-shirt a marine green, pinched one eye closed in that grizzled way he had, then pursed one side of his lip and spoke out of the other. "Navy man, my girl says."

Colin squared his shoulders and looked the man directly in the eye. "Yes, sir. I'm out of the service now in order to attend college and get my master's degree, but I plan to reenlist upon my ordination to the ministry."

"Good man," the sergeant barked, clapping Colin on the back. "Rather you were a marine, but military's always welcome under this roof."

Colin grinned as casual as ever. "Thank you, sir. I'm glad to be here."

"Mrs. McCade will be sorry she missed the chance to be here to greet you, but she had some last-minute shopping to do." Sergeant McCade grunted. "Put a roast in the oven and took off like a whirlwind. Don't know what got in her craw."

Holly giggled and shared an amused look with Colin. She had told him a little bit about her sweet, quixotic mother, and it was just like her to run off at the last minute for some frivolous reason or another when she had guests coming.

She probably wanted to impress Colin, Holly thought, smothering another laugh. Impress him with a new red-checked tablecloth, or turkey-shaped salt shakers or Mother-only-knew what else.

More likely, when her mother did finally see him,

Colin would be the one impressing *her*. It wasn't every day Holly brought a devastatingly handsome and charming man home to supper. Mom was in for a shocker.

With the tender consideration of a true gentleman, Colin placed a hand at the small of her back and accompanied her inside. Without hovering, he remained close to her side, his broad shoulders serving as a protective and very effective barrier between Holly and her father until she was ready to face him.

"Hello to you, too, Daddy," Holly said, giving Ian a perfunctory hug and a kiss on the cheek. He looked older than she remembered, and tired.

Or maybe *she* was the one feeling old and tired. At this point it was hard to tell.

"Sweet Pea."

She blushed at the use of her father's pet name for her. If he was trying to embarrass her, he was doing a wonderful job of it.

"Holly, why don't you go on down to your room, and I'll bring your things along to you shortly. Colin, grab your gear and follow me. I'm putting you up in the spare room."

He paused and looked back severely. "The one on the *opposite* end of the house from Holly, if you take my meaning."

Colin chuckled, but his smile, for once, did not reach his face. His blue eyes were like ice cubes. "That will be fine, sir."

Holly held back in astonishment that Colin didn't bark back at her father for such insensitivity. He'd had no right, and Colin was his own man.

Sure, he was easygoing, but no man enjoyed being pushed around, and she thought Colin, most of all, would get his back up at being ordered about.

She half expected—*hoped,* she recognized suddenly—that Colin would stand up to her father in the way she'd always wanted to but never had the nerve.

Instead, he was rigidly polite, and clearly military. To his credit, he didn't say a word when provoked, except a brisk, military sanction.

Still, it could happen. Her drill sergeant father was a master at provocation, and Holly was pretty sure he wouldn't let up on Colin, if for no other reason than that she had brought him home.

Hit the right button, and every man would go off.

Even cool, cavalier Colin Brockman.

Colin was obviously a master at maintaining his composure, or else he had an arctic demeanor that was a part of him she hadn't seen before. Evidently, he had some way of shielding his true thoughts and feelings from the world, more than just the carelessness or even world-weariness she'd observed in him earlier.

Had the military given him this rigid self-possession? Or had his youth—his father—cast these scars?

"Young man, there's another thing we'd best get

straight about your stay here,'' Ian continued, as if Colin's icy eyes weren't boring into him. ''Something very important. Pay attention.''

Holly tensed, anticipating the explosion. Either it would be her father's words, or Colin's temper.

''If I find you so much as in the same hallway as the one where my little girl sleeps, I'm going to tan your hide from here to Texas.''

Colin flashed a suddenly warm, amused glance in her direction before he grinned at the sergeant. This time, the smile was real, even a little bit cheeky. Holly knew it, and she knew her father knew it. ''Yes, sir, Sergeant McCade, sir. I understand completely, sir.''

''What?'' snapped the sergeant when Colin looked as if he wanted to say more.

''Well, sir, I was just thinking…''

''Get on with it.''

''You've warned me about visiting your daughter's hallway, sir.''

''What's your point?''

Colin's gaze met Holly's, his eyes sparkling. ''I think it's only fair that you warn her off mine. Or you'll tan *her* hide all the way from here to Texas?''

''Colin Brockman, you are treading on very thin water,'' Holly warned, holding out one hand and swinging her purse like a weapon.

''Are you being impertinent, son?'' Ian McCade asked at the same time.

"I dare you," Colin said to Holly, his eyes brimming over with laughter.

When his gaze shifted to her father, Holly took the opening and nailed him in the rib cage with her purse. Colin was on it in a moment, hooting with triumph as he wrapped the strap around his wrist. He used the momentum of the swing to yank Holly off balance and pull her under his arm, where he tucked her snugly.

"Yes, sir," he said, nodding at her father. "Completely impertinent."

The sergeant roared with laughter. "Glad to hear it. Welcome to the McCades, son. Home away from home."

Colin unpacked his bag and settled in to the small but comfortable room he'd been given. It was sparsely but tastefully decorated in masculine colors of red and blue. The twin bed looked a good deal more comfortable than the naval bunk to which he was accustomed, so he couldn't complain.

Keeping the room neat would be a trial, but not an impossibility. He'd managed in the navy, and he would manage now.

Using the small bathroom to wash up and run a comb through his already-tousled hair, he quickly adjourned to the den, where a roaring fire was blazing in the hearth. It was quiet, dark and cozy, and Colin found himself able to take his first real, deep breath in over an hour.

He covertly scanned the room. He could hear bustling sounds of pots and pans coming from the kitchen from whom he assumed was Mrs. McCade, and there was a black Labrador retriever dozing by the fire, but to his relief, Holly was nowhere around.

Colin had a mission to fulfill, and the sooner he got it over with, the better.

He'd realized as soon as he saw the stern, commanding drill sergeant that the older man had a noticeable soft spot in his heart for his little girl. But he highly doubted Holly had ever recognized that kind of affection from her father. Ian wasn't the effusive type, unless you called barking orders effusive.

For his part, Colin wasn't going to let himself be intimidated by the gruff old man—he'd seen enough hype in the military to know just what Sergeant McCade was trying to pull.

Colin grinned. A little bellowing wasn't going to keep him from asking Holly's gruff father a very important question.

Sergeant McCade was relaxing on a leather easy chair with his sock-covered feet propped up on a stool. He puffed with satisfaction on a black pipe, his black reading glasses propped on his nose as he perused the daily newspaper.

"Good afternoon, sir." He stood before the armchair as he greeted Holly's father, trying to be convincingly amicable and categorically unmilitary, knowing he succeeded at neither.

Ian grunted and waved toward the sofa, then buried his nose back in the newspaper.

Colin crouched on the edge of the cushion, elbows across his knees, his hands gripped tightly together. "I was wondering, sir, if I could talk with you. If you have a moment. If it's convenient."

He clamped his mouth shut before he said anything else stupid. Before he rambled anymore.

Sergeant McCade pinched the rim of his glasses between two fingers and pulled them halfway down his nose. For a moment, he merely eyed Colin over the rim, then grunted again and returned his glasses to the bridge of his nose, shaking his paper noisily.

Colin took that as a yes.

"Well, it's like this, sir," Colin began, tightly lacing his fingers in front of him. He was careful not to clench his fists. "Lately, I've been spending a lot of time with your daughter, and I want you to know I think the world of her."

Ian grunted harshly. "That so?"

"The truth is, I really like her. But I can't seem to get close to her. She's not the easiest person to reach. Maybe you know what I mean."

He cleared his throat, but found he couldn't look away from Sergeant McCade's stare. He was frozen to the spot, unable even to breathe.

Holly's marine drill sergeant father narrowed his

gaze on Colin the way a panther pinned down his prey. His eyes gleamed gray in the firelight. "Close."

"Close, sir, meaning getting to know her better, becoming good friends with her," Colin clarified, finding his breath, and his voice, with alacrity. "I want you to know up front that I'm a good Christian man, sir, and I'm committed to staying—" Colin felt himself stammering. "That is...being—"

Ian actually chuckled. Colin felt the tension ease from the room, and smiled back at the older man. Although he wasn't quite sure what Sergeant McCade found so funny in the situation. While Colin was sweating bullets, Ian was as cool as the proverbial cucumber.

"I get your point," the sergeant replied acerbically. "And while I don't know *why* I believe you, I do believe you."

"You do?" Colin asked in surprise, his face flushed with elation.

"Yes," Ian answered briskly. "I do." He steepled his fingers and tipped them to his chin. "So, then your problems concerning my daughter are merely in the...*spiritual* realm then? Is that correct?" he asked with an amused twist to his lip.

The flush in Colin's face increased until he was sure his skin was flaming red. He cleared his throat against the pressure choking him. "Uh, not exactly, sir."

"Meaning?"

"Yes...w-well." Colin stopped, realizing he was

stammering again. That would never do, not with a marine drill sergeant. He'd best just say it like it was and get it over with, since he'd come this far. "The fact is, sir, I kissed her."

Ian didn't budge. Colin expected him to frown, or chuckle or shoot him dead right there on the spot. Ian was a rock, showing not an ounce of emotion.

He did have a few words, however.

"What about your commitment to—" Ian cleared his throat, a little overdramatically, if you asked Colin, but then, drill sergeants were given to the overdramatic.

"Frankly, sir," Colin said, deciding to be blunt, "it seemed like the right thing to do at the time. As a general rule, I don't see anything wrong with stealing a kiss now and again."

"And is that what you did?" Ian's words were straight and wry. Still no bona fide reaction, though, not even in his expression. His gray eyes were as cold as ever. "*Steal* a kiss?"

Colin thought back to the moment he'd kissed Holly, how she'd melted into his arms, how right it felt to hold her and feel her heart beat with his.

"Yes, sir," he said at last. She *had* reacted, but he hadn't given her any hint of his intentions. He'd shoulder the responsibility.

"There's your problem," Ian said with the solemn authority of a father. He steepled his fingers again and looked wise—and unapproachable.

"What's that?" Colin asked, confused. "My problem is that I kissed your daughter? That sounds like just the sort of advice a woman's father would give."

Suddenly the rock broke. Amusement spilled like a water from a broken dam from Ian's gray eyes. "No, young man. Pay attention to what I'm saying. Your problem is that you *stole* a kiss. Like a thief."

Colin's eyebrows met the crook of his nose. "I don't understand."

Ian chuckled. "No, you certainly don't, my boy." He ran a grizzled hand over his wrinkled, clean-shaven cheek. "I think maybe you don't know my Holly well enough to be kissing her."

Colin bristled. "I know her well enough. And if she'd let me—"

Ian silenced him, laying a fatherly hand on Colin's sweatered shoulder and giving it a squeeze. "Take it from her father, my boy," he said in a surprisingly gentle tone. "Holly doesn't want to be trifled with by any young man, most especially a man in uniform."

"Trifled with? Oh, but, sir—"

"I know, son. But trust me. She doesn't see things the way you and I do." He pinched his lips together tightly, obviously pausing in order to choose his words wisely and thoughtfully.

After a moment, he continued. "She's had some—bad experiences in her life."

Colin frowned.

"I'm sure she'll tell you about them when she's ready for you to know. But do yourself a favor in the meantime. Don't steal any more kisses."

"Sir, I would never trifle with Holly." His voice was an octave lower than normal. He was surprised by the fervency burning in his heart, how much he meant what he was saying.

Where had this strength of emotion come from?

He would never have guessed he had it in him, to feel like this. It was a invigorating revelation, but a sober one.

He'd never expected this conversation to take such a serious tone. Nor for his heart to have taken such a serious turn.

He squared his shoulders and looked Ian straight in the eye. "I wouldn't hurt Holly. Not ever. You have my word on that."

"Good." Ian nodded firmly. "But don't tell *me*. Tell Holly."

He swept in an audible breath and turned his gaze away, looking distant for a moment before returning to the present.

He gave Colin a grimace that was an old man's close rendition of a smile. "Holly is good at keeping things deep inside that pretty head of hers, but I can guarantee you she's worrying about it."

"I'll get right on it, sir." Colin stood and nodded at the grizzled soldier, feeling almost as if he should salute.

"Don't push her."

"No, sir."

Ian leaned back in his chair and returned his pipe

to his mouth. As he fluffed his paper back to where it had been, he spoke one more time.

"You're the kind of man Holly needs in her life, sailor. A man who faces up to his challenges."

Colin nodded to the older man, but since the sergeant was clearly already engrossed in the newspaper, he decided to go back to his room. As he walked, he mulled over what Ian McCade had said about facing up to challenges.

Colin had been faced with many challenges in his lifetime. Now, with God's help and a great deal of his own determination, he had faced up to every challenge he'd encountered, even the lingering pain of his father's mental abuse, which he knew would never quite leave him alone.

But this—this was new to him.

Being with Holly was a challenge unlike any other he had faced. He paused in the hallway and closed his eyes for a moment, restoring his equilibrium and evening his breath.

He smiled, knowing what lay before him would be worth whatever effort he had to expend; for winning the love of a woman, Colin thought, his chest swelling with newly hatched emotion, must truly be the biggest challenge a man would ever face.

And the biggest triumph he would ever know.

Chapter Ten

Holly didn't remember a Thanksgiving dinner quite as unusual and uncomfortable as this one was turning out to be. She shifted in her seat, vitally aware of the energy crackling in the air. The tension was so thick she thought she might be able to reach up with her hand and touch it, and be physically shocked by the sheer electricity of the moment.

Her father had asked—though it had sounded more of a gruff command than a question, coming from her father's lips—for Colin to say the grace.

The request was met with a smile, as Holly knew it would be. Everyone knew he was a future navy chaplain. This was probably the first of many such requests.

Colin's prayer was simple and elegant, but the words he spoke had Holly wondering what planet she was on. Were these people really her parents? Was the grinning man sitting across from her really the man she had brought home for the holidays?

Thanking the Lord for food, family and friends had been what Holly considered in the normal realm of things, typical Thanksgiving fare. But then Colin started going off on the oddest tangent—something about thanking God for people who chose to forgive, to give old friends a second chance at friendship, and how precious they were in the eyes of God.

She could have sworn she heard her father smothering a laugh.

Her stern, taskmaster father laughing during prayer?

Impossible!

She looked from one stiff-spined military man to the other, but could find no clues in their expressions. She picked at her meal, no longer feeling hungry.

She didn't like the notion she was missing out on some kind of inside joke between everyone else. What was going on in this house?

Colin didn't appear to have any misgivings about his own meal. He greedily gulped down enormous bites of food, between equally large quantities of conversation. He appeared completely at ease with her parents, much more so than she herself felt at the moment.

Or ever, for that matter.

And her father was watching her. She could feel

his eyes upon her whenever Colin was speaking. But if he thought to intimidate her or make her feel funny for bringing Colin home, he'd have to think again.

She reminded herself that she was no longer the small girl trying to win her daddy's approval. She had nothing to prove here today. She was simply eating a holiday meal with the family.

And she'd brought a friend home with her this year. Her mother, at least, was pleased by Colin's obvious enthusiasm for everything around him, the food and gracious company most especially.

Holly put her fork to her plate and decided the best course of action was to concentrate on her food and let the other details worry about themselves. It was hard to swallow at times, especially whenever Colin looked her way.

All through the meal, it seemed to Holly that Colin was sending her silent messages with his smile, but she had no idea what he had on his mind. She wasn't about to ask him out loud.

Not at the dinner table. And not with her father present. He'd tell her in his own good time, whatever it was that was pressing on him.

She didn't have long to wait. When her mother rose from the table and began stacking the plates, Colin charged into action, charmingly and literally disarming her mother of the dishes, insisting he would do them on his own, since he was the guest.

Holly rose, intending to follow his lead, but he shook his head. "No, no. No dishes for you."

But when she turned away, he was equally as adamant. "No, no. Don't leave. Follow me," he said as he led her into the kitchen. "I just want you to sit and keep me company," he explained as he dropped the dishes onto the counter with a clatter, scraped out a stool from the breakfast bar and gestured her into it.

"What's this about?" she asked as he filled the sink with hot, sudsy water.

He shrugged and set a stack of dirty plates in the water. "I just thought I should do a little bit to help out, since your mom spent the whole day in the kitchen creating that fantastic culinary masterpiece we just consumed."

"That's not what I was talking about, and you know it."

Colin didn't answer.

She changed the subject. "I expect my father is happily ensconced on his favorite chair in the family room by now, puffing on that silly old pipe of his. I've tried to get him to quit, but he's a stubborn son of a gun."

Colin didn't answer, busy as he was scrubbing at the dishes. It was amazing how masculine he looked, his sleeves pushed up, and hunkered over a sink of dirty dishes, a towel slapped over his shoulder.

She shook her head and laughed softly, resuming

her soliloquy. "And if I know my mom, she will be sitting at his side, cross-stitching or reading a novel. They've had the same after-dinner routine for as many years as I can remember. It was one of those odd family habits that made life feel the same, even when we moved around the world as a military family. They always made me do the dishes, which I highly resented, of course. Just Dad, Mom and me. Funny, how I remember it so clearly just now."

"I've been smoking this pipe longer than you've been alive, missy," Colin mimicked in a surprisingly accurate rendition of her father, from his low, scratchy voice, all the way down to how he pinched one eye and half of his mouth closed as he talked.

Holly laughed, truly delighted. Her throat was still tight with emotion, but Colin's antics had helped. At least now she could swallow.

Colin chuckled with her, then nodded as he wiped a plate clean. "I've seen him puffing at that old pipe. He's a man with a mission. I don't think I'd want to mess with that kind of dedication."

"When did you see my father with his pipe?" she asked, surprise jolting through her at the odd sensation that something was not quite right.

She hadn't seen Colin and her father together a handful of times since they'd arrived at the lodge; and then never in the den, which was the only place her mother allowed her father to smoke his pipe.

"I saw him with his pipe at the same time he told

me why you're so afraid of me,'' Colin said, his voice soft and even.

Holly blanched. "What?"

Her father had told Colin about her teen years? When she'd rebelled against God and everyone? When she'd run with a loose crowd, both figuratively and literally?

He wouldn't do that to her. Would he?

"I don't believe you."

"It was a good conversation, Holly. We both felt it was very productive."

She stood and turned away from Colin, grasping the back of a chair for support. How could her father betray her trust in so cruel a manner?

And why to *Colin?*

Why not just blare it out over the military megaphone to the whole world and have it over with?

All she'd struggled to build through the years was crumbling down around her in a big messy heap. This was her worst nightmare come true.

Colin knew the truth. He had *sought out* the truth. But she couldn't blame him.

She was the one living a lie.

"He told you all about me, then," she acknowledged, her voice sounding flat to her own ears. But better flat than panicked.

"I already knew everything I need to know about you before I ever talked to your father, Holly McCade," he whispered softly, just next to her ear.

Somehow he'd moved behind her without her knowing. His steady, warm breath both soothed and ruffled her at the same time.

Holly closed her eyes tightly. She couldn't bear to think of Colin picturing her at the height of her immaturity, and she certainly didn't want to see the look on his face right now.

But she'd always known she couldn't hide the truth forever. Purity was something she'd embraced in her early twenties, too late to take back that precious gift God gave only once between a man and a woman.

She'd desperately wanted to believe the lie, as a teenager, that love and sex were the same thing. By the time she'd realized the truth, it was too late to turn back the clock.

If she ever were to marry, it would have to be to a man with a big heart.

Like Colin.

Her own thoughts burned through her. She hadn't realized…hadn't recognized…

"He didn't tell me any state secrets," Colin assured her, running his palms across her shoulders before turning her firmly around to face him. "He was helping me with *my* problem."

"And what would that be?" Holly blurted, eager to turn the spotlight away from herself, even if it were only for a moment. The rush of relief she felt was on an equal par with her curiosity to know what he considered his own quandaries.

"Well...*you*," he admitted wryly as he grinned down on her.

"Me. Since when did I become a problem?"

"Holly, what do you want out of life?" he asked, answering a question with a question.

"More than I can probably get." She looked away, ashamed of the cynical streak that ran through her, but unable to take back the words.

"Meaning?"

She let out an audible sigh. "What most women want, I suppose. A husband. A dozen kids. A home of my own to keep them in."

"With a lock on the bathroom so you can find some privacy," Colin inserted, the gleam in his eyes both teasing and caring.

"That, too." She chuckled.

"What else?"

"What else? Oh, I don't know. The usual. A career. I want to help people, you know?"

He tucked her under his chin and held her there against his chest, where she could hear the strong, even beating of his heart. "Yeah, I know."

"Isn't that what you want?" she asked quietly, her voice muffled against the softness of his sweater. "A home? A family? Eventually, I mean."

She felt his muscles stiffen, though he didn't move away. She slid her arms around his waist and gave him a strong hug.

"I somehow don't think that's what God's got

planned for me,'' he said, and she could hear the tension in his voice.

''Why is that?''

He pushed her away from him enough that he could gaze down into her eyes. ''You know better than anyone how bad the military lifestyle is on children. I wouldn't be so brutal as to subject my own kids to that kind of torture, never mind my wife.''

''It doesn't have to be that way.'' She was amazed by the words coming from her own mouth; yet in the same moment, she knew what she said was true.

Her own experiences as a child of military parents didn't preclude the possibility of someone else making it work. And she and Colin had turned out all right despite the problems.

She could make it work.

She could raise military children. She already knew all the pitfalls. She could avoid them herself, and help her own children over the humps.

Of course she would never admit such a thought, most especially not to Colin.

He had returned to the sink and was noisily stacking dishes. His back to her, she covertly admired his broad shoulders and muscular physique.

''Do you think I trifle with you?'' Colin didn't give any indication he'd spoken. His words were so low and velvety soft that it was almost as if he hadn't spoken at all.

But that didn't stop the bolt of electricity that

sparked through her at his words, nor the heat rising to stain her cheeks in protest.

"Trifle? What do mean, *trifle?* Who uses a word like *trifle* these days?"

The answer hit her just as Colin turned, looking at once amused and sheepish. She blushed to the roots of her hair.

"Colin Brockman, *what* has my father been telling you?"

Chapter Eleven

A week later, Colin still wasn't sure how he'd gotten out of Holly's query about her father without losing his humor or his head, though Holly had threatened both and more.

But now that he was tightly ensconced in his own comfortable—if messy—apartment, he could relax, even if he couldn't quite forget about the close call. He was sprawled on the floor in front of the coffee table, a large, daunting stack of papers and books spread around him.

He had no idea where he should start. The ominous pile gave him a gut feeling that was at least as over-whelming as the one he'd experienced in his first week in boot camp. Only, this time, there was no one yelling in his face to get the job done.

He was so far behind on his studies that he thought

he might never be able to catch up. It was amazing what a pretty face could do to a man's mind. Last weekend, at Holly's parents' lodge, his mind had been on Holly alone. He hadn't even thought to crack a book.

Now, when he knew he had to either get with the program or face the consequences, he was *still* having trouble concentrating, keeping his mind off a certain sable-haired beauty with velvet-green eyes that made a man's insides turn to mush.

He flipped open the book on the top of the pile and tried to read, but he couldn't help reminiscing, even so.

It had been an amazing weekend. Sitting with Holly's mom and dad and having a real old-fashioned holiday meal had been the highlight. That, and his talk with Ian, who had shed some light on Colin's relationship with Holly.

He was especially grateful to Gwen, Holly's mom, who had come into the kitchen to see how the dishes were progressing. If she hadn't stepped in at just the right moment, Colin may have been forced to reveal his hand.

And he hadn't studied his cards yet.

He grinned and chuckled. How providential could a man get?

He'd slipped away without having to say a word. Without answering Holly's query on the word *trifle*.

Without admitting how far her father's conversation had gone, how much he now had to think about.

For in truth, he was beginning to think seriously about Holly, wondering if God might have meant for her to be his life's partner. The Man Who Would Be Single was now contemplating matrimony—if not seriously, then at least with some degree of significance.

Marriage.

It wasn't as frightening a concept now that Holly was in his life. If it wasn't for his own fear—that of becoming a man like his father—he'd probably have whisked her off to the altar already.

Any sane man would have.

He chuckled under his breath and tossed aside the book he'd been reading. He picked up the next book nearest his reach. Sliding down to one elbow on the carpet, he yawned widely and forced himself to open the book, wishing not for the first time that he was a better student.

Though he'd never gotten much above C's and B's in high school, he knew he could be a good student if he put his mind to it. If he'd learned one thing during his years in the military, it was that he could improve himself, but he had to work harder.

He creased his brow, determined to buckle down.

He'd found his spot in the history book he held, and had read maybe three-quarters of a page when there was a knock on his door.

He groaned. Was he doomed to fail the semester?

He was never going to be able to follow his dream of becoming a chaplain this way.

"Just a second," he hollered as he rolled to his feet. He half staggered to the door on legs that had fallen asleep on him, muttering under his breath about not being as young as he used to be.

Still grumbling, he yanked at the knob, determined to send whoever was on the other side of the door running for cover, so he could get back to the mind-numbing tediousness of his own work.

But when he opened the door, all thoughts of books and study were swept from his mind by the sight of Holly, her eyes sparkling with excitement. She shifted, almost bounced, from foot to foot, clearly in anticipation of the words that looked like they were about to bubble right out of her mouth.

Colin grinned and gestured her in. He'd never seen Ms. Straight-Arrow like this, and to say his interest was piqued would have been an understatement.

She made it two steps inside the door before she ruptured.

"Oh, Colin, I'm so excited," she burst out, whirling to pull him in the doorway and close the door. She gave him an impromptu hug that sent them both careening, until he uprighted them with a good show of strength.

He laughed loudly and swung her around. "I can see that. What gives?"

"You won't believe it."

"Why don't you sit down and tell me about it? Do you want a soda or something?"

Holly took off her coat tossed a load of books from an armchair to the floor. "A cola would be great, thanks. With ice, if you have it."

"Coming right up. Make yourself comfortable."

"There's plenty of padding," she teased, "what with all these socks and jackets lying around."

"What?" he squawked in protest. "But I cleaned this week."

Her high, tinkling laughter filled the air, and his throat closed tightly. She sounded like a spring fairy, flittering from flower to flower and laughing joyfully all the while.

Of course, if he told Holly what he was thinking, she'd probably want to crack him alongside the head with a two-by-four. Flittering and fairy weren't probably how she would want to be described.

She was a modicum of decorum, or at least a sleek, contemporary career woman.

Not the flittering type.

Colin grabbed a soda for Holly and one for himself, then kicked the refrigerator door shut with his bare foot and went back and settled himself on the couch, his legs propped on an empty corner of the coffee table.

"So what's up?" he asked with a grin.

Holly took a deep breath, and then let it out audibly. "I've found it!"

"It?" Colin parroted, popping the top on Holly's soda and pouring the bubbling liquid in a tall, ice-filled glass.

Holly looked at him as if he were dense. "Your theme paper. It's practically written itself, thanks very much to me."

"I'm interested." He slid a glance toward the gaping pile of yet-to-be-read books on his floor. Boy, was he interested.

Holly reached out and stroked his arm. "I thought you would be."

"Go on."

"Well, it's like this," she began, as if starting an epic tale.

"Once upon a time…" he teased.

"You'll think it's a fairy tale by the time I'm finished," she promised. "Anyway, to get back to the story, I went to church on Sunday."

"How very pious of you."

"Colin!"

He frowned, trying to look penitent and humble. Kind of. He cleared his throat on a chuckle. "Sorry."

"I'm sure. Now let me get on with the story. When I attended church last Sunday, they had a special program during the service. St. Andrew's does that sometimes, in order to motivate our parishioners to be out *doing* things for God in the world instead of just sitting in the pew thinking about good works. Pastor Freeman is a firm believer in acting out one's faith."

"Good man," Colin agreed. "Not enough people walking the talk."

Holly laughed. "You almost sound like a preacher, Colin Brockman."

"I do?" he said, genuinely and pleasantly surprised. Maybe there was hope for him, yet.

"I haven't even gotten to the good part yet. The program Pastor Freeman introduced last week is called Kids Hope," she continued, smiling. "And it's the answer to your prayers. You can thank me now or later," she teased, laughter glimmering in her green eyes.

"Kids Hope," Colin repeated, smiling just because she did. "Sounds interesting. Tell me more."

He hated to be a pessimist, but deep down, he really didn't really think she had the answer. He was becoming more and more convinced there was no answer. He'd certainly been scoping around for one, and had even tried to come up with a few unique ideas of his own, all to no avail.

Still, he didn't want to spoil her fun, so he smiled his encouragement for her to continue.

"The program joins one organization, in this case my church, St. Andrew's Church, to one public school in their area, again, in this case, Stonington Elementary, which is just down the street from the church.

"At that point, the local executive director pairs adult mentors one-on-one with a child the teachers and parents believe would benefit from this service. The adult and the child meet for an hour every week. And every adult mentor is methodically supported by a prayer partner from the church.''

Colin felt pinpricks of excitement brush over his skin as energy pulsed through his veins. Could Holly be on to something? "One-on-one, you said?"

"Exactly. That's the difference. The key. Do you see what I see?"

He did. His head was swimming with the possibilities. "How do you think something like this would work out on a military base?"

"Uh, Colin, that would be for you to figure out. Do you want me to write and type your term paper for you, too, or what?"

He ignored her teasing sarcasm, and hooted in delight. "What a breakthrough! I need to start by getting the lowdown on the basic training maneuvers, and move on from there. Do you suppose I could get an appointment with your pastor anytime soon?"

Holly patted both her knees with her palms. "Done. Thursday at 4:00 p.m. I hope that time will work for you. I wasn't sure of your schedule."

Colin squared his shoulders and widened his grin. "I'll *make* it okay. I can't believe you've done this for me. You're an angel."

He stood and extended his arms to help her to her feet. She stood slowly, almost hesitantly. He didn't let go of her hands, choosing instead to run his thumbs across the soft skin behind her fingers.

Their eyes met, and her gaze softened, but she took a single step backward, shifting ever so slightly, putting the subtlest line of distance between them.

"You're a dream," he said huskily.

"Bad or good?" she quipped as she shifted from one foot to another. She didn't quite look at him—meeting his gaze and then looking away.

He wondered what he had done to make her nervous in his presence. But even he could feel the underlying electricity in the air.

Maybe that was it. His heart was buzzing with the exhilaration of the moment, and he could imagine her heart in sync with his.

He raised her hands to his lips and brushed light kisses across the softness of her knuckles. "You're the best kind of dream," he assured her, smiling into her warm, velvet eyes. "A fantasy."

Mere inches separated them. He lowered his head to keep their gazes locked. "Is it okay that I dream about you, Holly?"

A chuckle escaped her lips, but her fingers quivered when he asked the question.

"If I can dream about you," she whispered after a long pause.

The air was suddenly thick with tension, and Colin struggled to pull in a breath. "I wouldn't have it any other way."

He found himself drawn toward her, his gaze wandering to her gloss-shined lips. He wondered if she was dwelling on the word *trifle*.

He hoped not. Because he could no more stop from kissing her than he could make the sun move backward in the sky.

As it happened, though, he didn't have to stop, or even make the first move. Holly, in a sudden impetuous move, put her arms around his neck, grabbed him by the collar and pulled his face down to hers, leaning toward him until their breath mixed.

"Kiss me." Barely a whisper, it was half a request, half a demand.

Colin willingly complied with both. With the utmost awareness, he leaned down and brushed his lips over hers, closing his eyes as he savored the sweet, gentle contact. His senses heightened at the same moment his world focused, until there was only the taste, sight, sound, smell and feel of Holly in his arms.

He closed his eyes, wanting the moment to last forever.

Instead, the atmosphere was instantly and completely shattered by the sound of the telephone ringing. Its shrill clang jolted through Colin's brain like a spoon on a frying pan, effectively dousing his romantic mood.

Even so, he didn't move or pull away, determined despite the disturbance not to lose the moment. He knew it might be a long time before they would reach such a point again.

Holly, however, immediately attempted to push back and break their embrace, turning aside toward the sound of the telephone.

"No," Colin protested, pulling her back into his arms. "Just ignore it."

Holly looked at the telephone, and then him. It was only a moment before she made her decision, melting back into his arms with a contented sigh, just as the answering machine picked up.

"This is a message for Colin Brockman," the woman on the line began. "This is Michelle Walker, the principal at Marston House. I need to speak to you as soon as possible regarding Jared Matthews."

Colin launched toward the telephone, but was too late to intercept the call. With his heart beating in his ears, he flashed an apologetic look toward Holly, tucked the receiver under his chin and rapidly punched out the numbers Michelle had recited.

Please, God, don't let him miss her.

Holly moved to his side and placed a hand on his shoulder, offering instant and silent support. He glanced down at her, flashing her a grateful smile.

She smiled softly in return.

"This is Colin Brockman," he said when Michelle answered, clearing his throat when he realized how low his voice sounded.

"Colin! I'm glad you called back so quickly," she

blurted immediately. "I'll cut to the chase. There is a problem with Jared Matthews, and I thought, under the circumstances, that you should know."

"What kind of problem with Jared?" Colin clenched his fist around the phone cord as his throat constricted around his breath, with emotion for the boy he'd come to love.

"I'd prefer to discuss it with you in person, if you don't mind." Her voice was firm, but clearly anxious, and Colin paced back and forth as far as the telephone cord would reach.

"I'll be right over."

He hung up the telephone and reached for his coat. "I'm sorry, Holly. I really want to discuss this whole Kids Hope thing with you, but it will have to wait until later. I'm afraid I have to leave right now. I'll walk you out."

Holly didn't say a word as he helped her into her coat, pulling it tight against her chin, since it was snowing outside, and wrapping her scarf firmly around her delicate neck, against the drafts.

"What's wrong with Jared?" she asked at last, halting him from his erratic movements with a level hand on his elbow.

"I don't know," he answered hoarsely. "Not something good, I'm afraid. I'm sure going to find out as soon as I can."

"I'm going with you," said Holly resolutely as he,

equally resolutely, pressed her out the door ahead of him, pausing only to lock the door.

He was about to assure her Jared wasn't her problem, at least not on this day. She should go home where it was warm, not follow him about in the cold chill of the winter afternoon. But something in the look she gave him stopped him from saying a word.

She was *making* it her problem. Because of *him*. Because of what they shared between them.

Again, his throat clouded with emotion. He had already been through a lot today, and he had the feeling the day wasn't over, not by a long shot.

Had it only been a few months ago that he hadn't been attached to a single person in the whole world? He'd been so proud of the fact that he was his own man, all alone with no one to care for, or to care for him.

How had he ever lived that way?

First there was his sister and her new family. And then there was Holly. And Jared. What was a man to do with himself?

He slid a glance toward the beautiful, loving woman at his side. He might not be sure what to do with himself, but he knew *exactly* what to do with her. He kept an arm around her waist as they left.

Together.

Chapter Twelve

Holly was surprised and pleased at how quickly Colin gave in to her request to accompany him.

Before he'd had the opportunity to send her away, she'd already mentally lined her arguments up in a row.

She'd been the one to introduce him to Marston House in the first place. She knew Jared and his case. And, the clincher, she hoped: *She was a child psychologist,* after all. A professional in her field. Perhaps she could be of some help.

And she'd needed none of it. Colin wanted her to be there. With him. For his own reasons.

He didn't speak the whole way to the school, but she didn't begrudge him the silence. She could tell his mind was on the meeting ahead. So she kept her hands folded on her lap and tried not to think about all the bad things Michelle Walker's telephone call could mean.

His small blue truck was a lot newer, and a good deal fancier, than her Jeep. It held in heat much better, and had a much nicer ride.

It was funny how she'd driven a Jeep all her life, just because her father's gift to her when she'd earned her driver's license had been a Jeep.

It was one of her best memories. Learning to drive had meant something to her father. He had been so proud of her that day.

She shook herself quickly to the present. Despite the smooth ride, Colin looked like he was bouncing all over—internally, at any rate. His square jaw was locked so tight she could see a tendon straining against his cheek. And he was scowling, something so foreign to Colin, it made Holly want to cringe.

She couldn't stand seeing him look so miserable. His boyish good looks set in a frown broke her heart. It was just *wrong*.

Slowly, so as not to startle him from his thoughts, she leaned toward him, stroking his brow, gently soothing the anxiety marked there.

"Thanks," he said gruffly.

"For what?"

"For being here. With me."

She choked up. "Where else would I be?"

He tossed a grin her direction, but it wasn't more

than a decent attempt, and came off more like the grimace he must be feeling inside.

She took his hand and squeezed.

They arrived at Marston House a moment later, and Colin parked, got out of the vehicle and quickly moved around the truck to get Holly's door. He lifted a hand to help her down from the truck, then linked her fingers with his as they entered the school, sending her the silent message that he needed her, that they were in this together.

She squeezed his hand, offering what little support she could. She was only beginning to realize how important Jared was to Colin, and her respect for the man grew with every moment, causing her throat to tighten as emotion swelled.

There weren't too many men who would put themselves forward for the sake of a helpless little boy, especially a boy like Jared who had special needs.

There weren't too many men like Colin Brockman.

Colin wasn't in Marston House a moment before he'd obviously spotted Jared. With a quick glance down at Holly, he lit off for the playroom where he'd first met Jared. Holly followed.

The boy had climbed up a pile of boxes and was sitting high in one corner of the room, curled up in a ball and looking as if the world didn't exist for him as he rocked back and forth, back and forth, staring into space and mumbling something unintelligible— and repeatedly.

Michelle put an arm around both adults as she entered the room. Frowning, Colin shook her hand off and started for the boy, clearly intent on finding out firsthand what was going on.

The principal stopped him. "Wait, Colin. I know you want to go to Jared, but there are some things you need to know first."

"What things?" Holly asked. It was heartrending, watching the child's visible agony.

"Jared got some bad news this morning. He's been like this all day," Michelle explained gravely. "Our staff hasn't been able to get through to him at all. I thought of you immediately, Colin. I know you've spent a good amount of time with Jared. I'm hoping maybe he'll respond to you."

Colin's troubled gaze met Holly's for a moment, and then he bowed his head. "I'm no expert. I don't know if I can help. But I'll do my best, ma'am."

Holly realized as she watched Colin approach Jared that he hadn't even waited to find out what had happened to send Jared into a downward spiral, though that was clearly a major concern. What could have happened to make Jared revert as he had?

They would find out in due time, she supposed. In the meantime, she'd take her cue from Colin. His first and only consideration was to be with the boy.

Tears pooled in the corner of Holly's eye, and she absently wiped them away. How many men would have made such an emotional commitment to a complete stranger?

Michelle approached Jared first, but when she laid her hand on his shoulder, he brushed her away with a near-violent jerk of his shoulder. She backed away from the boy with her hands held open, giving Colin a chance to crawl up the boxes and move in.

At first Colin merely crouched near Jared, speaking softly all the while, so the boy would know he was there, but not touching him or encroaching on his personal space.

He talked continually and watched unremittingly for a long while, but he didn't shift a muscle, though the minutes wore on.

Colin sat without moving for so long Holly began to wonder if Jared would respond to him, but Colin looked confident, if concerned. He somehow appeared to know instinctively that he needed to wait the boy out, to prove his trust and friendship by his presence and not by his touch.

Any concern he might be feeling in his heart didn't show in his voice. His low, steady baritone assured even Holly, as she listened to the quiet, soothing monotone whispering nonsensically.

Lost in her own thoughts, Holly missed the moment when contact was made, but suddenly the boy was in Colin's arms, rocking back and forth and making heartbreaking little rhythmic sounds that were a lot like sobs.

Colin's gaze met hers, and together they shared a moment of grief. Jared's cry was enough to break anyone's heart; and right now, Holly distinctively heard *two* hearts fracturing.

Colin resisted the urge to move. He wanted to tighten his grip on the little boy, but he knew instinctively it would be the wrong thing to do. Jared needed the kind of tenderness Colin thought that, with his own big, bumbling body and huge hands, he might not be able to give the small boy.

Yet, it was clear Jared was responding to him, and that, at least warmed his heart.

Jared had come to *him*.

He felt a great deal of responsibility toward the boy, but for some reason that burden didn't frighten him the way he thought it should have, or even would have as short as six months ago.

Had turning thirty somehow made him grow up, mature in some way he'd missed in the past?

Or maybe it was a combination of things—joining the navy, coming to know Christ, deciding to become a chaplain, meeting Holly and then getting to know Jared. Maybe it was a combination of life's events that caused a youth to become a man.

Whatever it was, he was just glad he had what it took to make the adult decisions and adult commitments it was clear he was going to have to make. At least he was beginning to believe he had what it took.

For Jared's sake, he hoped so.

"What happened to him, to set him back?" he asked Michelle quietly.

"You know he's been in foster care for several years," Michelle said gravely.

"Yes. You mentioned that you couldn't find a good fit for him, that he'd been in several homes over that period of time. Is that what's happening now?"

"Worse than that, I'm afraid," Michelle confirmed, her voice low.

Colin's gaze slid to Holly. She put her palms together and linked her fingers in front of her as their eyes met. Her message was clear.

We're in this together.

He took a deep breath and nodded. Somehow he felt better, just knowing Holly was there.

"His mother and father have abandoned him to the state," Michelle stated without preamble. "He's now officially an orphan."

"How could they?" Holly whispered harshly, her outrage showing clearly on her flushed face. "I've never heard of parents intentionally abandoning their children to the state. Can they do that? What kind of people would do that, anyway?"

Michelle sighed. "Welcome to the world of child psychology. Mothers and fathers don't always act the way you would expect them to, especially when their children have some kind of disability."

"But to abandon them to the state? How can a mother give up her child?"

"Sometimes they believe they are doing what is best for the child, giving him to caregivers who know more about how to deal with him and treat his special needs than they do. Sometimes they just don't want the responsibility of a child who is 'different.'"

"But isn't there another way?" Holly asked, disagreeing with her scowl as well as her words. "I just can't see it."

"Maybe they are poor, Holly," Colin broke in, though he realized he was treading in deep water. He was speaking about something he knew less than nothing about, and was probably better off keeping his mouth shut.

Holly looked up at him, her big green eyes luminescent with unshed tears. "Be that as it may, I don't think I'll ever understand. Or forgive. To me, there isn't a good enough reason in the world."

Holly was quiet the whole ride back to Colin's apartment, and left for her own apartment as soon as they'd reached Colin's place.

Frankly, she didn't know what to say to Colin. He had been magnificent, and she couldn't even find words to tell him how she felt when she saw him holding little Jared in his arms.

But right now she had other things on her mind. Like how she was going to be a total failure in her chosen field. She'd not realized until the moment she'd seen Jared all curled up, helpless and alone in the world, just what being a child psychologist really meant.

What *helping children* really meant.

It meant she'd have to face the tough cases, ones that didn't work out according to the rules of the book, or even the rules of decent life.

She supposed she'd always known that, in theory, but seeing Jared so helpless today had been all too much reality for her. She'd handled some questionable cases for the state in her college internship, but Jared stepped beyond the realm of books and into the personal.

She *knew* this boy.

And it made a difference.

She held strong feelings for Jared. He wasn't just any little boy, he was someone she knew and cared about, and would wonder what happened to when tomorrow came around.

Was there any way she could look at Jared's mother and father and not want to scream at them, force them to do the right thing, to love and serve this little boy who was such a precious gift in the eyes of God?

She closed her eyes, half in prayer, half in pain. She knew there were many ways to view such a situation, and that the way the state, or any other agency she worked for might not see things her way.

Could she handle being told to do something she didn't believe in?

She searched her soul, and found she wasn't sure of the answer to that question. Her faith was beating strongly in her heart.

She could not and would not turn her back on God. The quintessential question *What Would Jesus Do?* entered her mind.

Except she didn't know the answer to the question this time around. The issue wasn't exactly cut out in black and white.

Did she keep on with her plans for the future, doing good wherever she could and making the most of every bad situation? Or did she look for another way to serve God and the world?

Was there a way she could use her skills and be true to her faith at the same time? But was that what Jesus meant when He said to go into all the world?

She's never been more confused.

There were other avenues for a trained child psychologist than working for the state. Some were overtly religious, though she'd never before considered such a vocation. Somehow, she didn't see herself as a missionary to the children in South Africa, but odder things had happened.

She wondered what Colin was thinking. Knowing Colin, he was probably out playing basketball or something, his problems already happily forgotten in the fluky, whimsical life he led.

She wished she could throw her own problems to the wind, but she knew that was beyond her capability. She was the proverbial stick in the mud. Her troubles were bound to follow her no matter where she went.

For her, the trick was to turn around and face them head-on.

Colin was not playing basketball. He wasn't playing anything. And he definitely had not been able to put aside his problems.

He slumped back in his chair, brought his hands to his head and brushed his fingers through his already tousled hair.

As soon as he'd dropped Holly off at her car, he'd turned his truck around and returned to Marston House. An idea had popped into his mind during the silent ride home with Holly, and he couldn't shake it no matter how he tried.

He'd spent a few minutes in silent, frantic prayer with God, almost begging to be talked out of the crazy idea. But when he'd felt that gentle nudging of God on his heart, he decided to follow up right away, before he lost his nerve. And that involved speaking to Michelle.

The principal of Marston House had been surprisingly receptive to his plan, but had soon excused herself to get some papers, and was taking forever to come back to her small, sparsely furnished office located at the far east end of the school.

Colin sighed and crossed his arms over his chest, his palms resting tightly over his upper torso.

This had been the longest, hardest day of his life. Even his first few days of navy basic training couldn't compare to the strain he was feeling now.

At boot camp, they battered his body; but today, holding Jared while he grieved, sheltering the precious little boy in his arms, was far worse agony than anything the navy could dole out.

Being with Jared battered his emotions, and more than that, struck at his very soul.

He'd heard Holly's anger when she lashed out at Jared's parents' actions, and he shared in that sentiment. But his mind had been so taken over with Jared's immediate needs, he hadn't wanted to waste any energy on emotion.

What he needed were solutions.

Another foster home wasn't going to be the answer for the boy. Even if he was sent to another home, he'd more than likely be permanently sent back to the state before long.

Maybe someone could reason with Jared's parents, but Colin doubted it. The boy's parents had obviously not come to their decision overnight, and it was doubtful more counseling would change their minds about what they felt they had to do, for whatever reasons they had for making the decisions they did.

Colin couldn't help but feel that Jared, with whatever understanding he had about what was going on around him and to him, was losing hope—in the system, in humankind, maybe even in God.

Colin grit his teeth and slammed his fist down on the tabletop. He couldn't let that happen to another young boy.

Not while he was there to stop it.

Chapter Thirteen

Holly wasn't sure why her father had called her up to his lodge over the weekend, but whatever it was, it couldn't be good. He'd used his drill sergeant voice when he'd spoken with her, so there was no room to brook an argument.

And her father had emphasized the need to hurry, too, so she hadn't said goodbye to Colin, or even let him know where she was going.

She was sorry she couldn't make contact, but when she'd called his apartment there'd been no answer; and of course, in typical Colin fashion, he hadn't remembered to turn on his answering machine.

Since they spent nearly every day together these days, she knew he would probably, and rightfully, assume they'd be spending the weekend together.

Which they would be, were it not for her father's request.

Even so, she knew Colin wouldn't be angry with her when he found out she was gone, even if he didn't know why or where she'd gone. He might worry a little bit, but it wasn't in his nature to stress over things the way she did, so she didn't worry—too much—that she'd caused him undue anxiety.

She had the oddest feeling, though, that it was a bad time to leave, a time when Colin really needed a friend by his side. She knew he was broken up over what had happened to Jared, even if he hadn't expressed his feelings to her.

For one thing, he'd reverted to his rigid, military posture and stiff upper lip, both literally and figuratively. That was enough to let Holly know something was seriously amiss in Colin's world.

And all the while he was wrestling with the situation with Jared, he was trying to pull things together with his Kid's Hope project for her class, which in itself was a huge undertaking. He'd been making phone calls and reading dozens of books, which she knew was not his favorite pastime.

He told her in confidence he was working on a PowerPoint presentation he could use after he graduated, even though she'd assured him he needn't go to *quite* that much effort for her class. He wanted something he could use on naval bases, and was proving himself a lot more focused than Holly would have thought.

She couldn't stop thinking about Colin the whole

hour's drive to the lodge, which was a surprise. She was still broken up about her own dilemma, to which she'd come to no decent conclusions.

More than that, she knew she ought to be pondering all the possible reasons why her parents might want to see her. At the very least she should be giving it a guess.

It could be that all they wanted to do was to lecture her about why she wasn't getting married and starting a family. Certainly, bringing Colin home for Thanksgiving might have sparked that old flame.

It was a tune she'd heard many a time before, especially from her mother, although why that should require an extra trip on Holly's part was beyond anything she could contrive.

The truth was, she couldn't think of a single reason why her parents would want to speak to her in person. A telephone call would do for most things she could conceive as a problem, and they could wait until her next visit on anything else they had to say.

Unless someone was sick. But that would mean *really* sick—fatally ill, even.

Her stomach lurched as she rolled the thought over in her head. She pulled the Jeep's steering wheel sharply to the left and slammed her foot on the brake as she executed a sharp hairpin curve on the washboard dirt road, and swallowed hard to gulp down her dismay.

Was her mother incurably sick? Had her dad, her

dear, gruff Marine Corps father, contracted some sort of serious illness?

No.

It couldn't be, and she wouldn't let herself consider it for another moment. If her foot came down a little bit harder on the gas pedal, it was purely coincidental.

And it was, fortunately, on a straight segment of road.

Despite promising herself she would do no such thing, Holly had thoroughly worked herself up by the time she'd reached the lodge, simply by *not* thinking about it. She dashed from the car, let herself into the front door and launched into her unsuspecting father's arms, her tears wetting his weather-hardened cheek and dripping onto the plain forest green of a marine-issue T-shirt.

He promptly pushed her aside, squaring his shoulders and frowning over her, though he still supported her with one arm.

"What's this, now?" he barked in his best drill sergeant voice. "Buck up, young lady. We'll have no crying here."

From habit learned in childhood, she straightened herself to military rigidity and wiped her eyes.

And it helped. She was oddly comforted by his gruff actions.

The familiarity of old habit soothed her, however rough it might seem to the outside world. This was a marine daddy with his little girl, and this was the way things ran in her world.

She knew better than to shed tears in her father's presence. In truth, she thought a woman's tears might be the one thing her tough old military father couldn't handle.

"Sorry," she scratched out, her throat dry.

"Done," her father replied with a snappy nod. He'd never been much of one for extended apologies. "But don't let your mother see you this way. You know how your tears upset her."

"Yes, sir." It warmed her heart at the way her father still protected her mother, as if the woman was made of fine china, and was not the strong, sweet woman who had devoted her life to him and was in truth, in many ways, stronger than he ever was.

"How is Mom?" she queried, hoping for information to confirm, or hopefully allow her to discard, her disturbing theories.

Her father's eyebrows creased, but his eyes sparkled with mirth. "Meddling as ever."

Her heart swam with relief, and her breath relaxed as her anxiety melted within her. "She's still trying to get you to quit smoking that pipe, huh?"

He grunted. "The never-ending battle. Maybe someday I'll just quit that old pipe cold turkey and send her into an apoplexy." He laughed good-naturedly. "But then we wouldn't have anything to fight about, and our marriage would be over."

Holly laughed with him. "It would be over? Why is that?"

He gazed at her solemnly, then ruined the impression with a sly wink. "Why, then, we'd have nothing left to talk about!"

Holly laughed with him. "Then neither one of you is ill."

"'Course not. I can't imagine where you'd get an idea like that."

She *could* imagine. And for once in her life, she was quite relieved to be wrong.

"Are you wondering why we called you down to the lodge?" he asked bluntly. "Because if that's what's bothering you, you don't have to get all in a snither about it." He picked up her suitcases and gestured her down the hallway.

She snorted her protest. "I'm not in a *snither,* Dad. But you have to admit you were rather vague about why you asked me to come up here this weekend. Is it some kind of surprise?"

He gave her a half grin and nodded. "You could say that."

For a man who spent his life being inordinately upfront with people, he sure was beating around the bush with her now.

"Is it for me? It's not my birthday," she reminded him. "Nor a holiday."

Her father looked about ready to speak when the doorbell rang. Since they'd stopped in the middle of the hallway in the intensity of their conversation, they hadn't quite made it all the way to Holly's bedroom to drop off her luggage.

In his typical, immediate military fashion, her father dropped the suitcases neatly in a row by the wall, and strode back toward the door with quick, even steps.

Curious, Holly followed, though she lagged behind her father's brisk pace. It really wasn't her business who was at the door—probably the milkman, or perhaps a neighbor calling.

"Colin," she exclaimed when her father opened the door and she caught a glimpse of the thatch-haired navy man standing in the doorway, his back ramrod straight, his broad shoulders even, the very picture of military stature.

Her heart immediately began pounding riotously at the sight of him, especially as much of a shock as it was to see him here.

The only thing to ruin the keen navy image he was obviously trying for, was the slow, lazy smile that appeared on his face. The very same grin that had driven Holly crazy a million times. The smile that said he had everything under control, and maybe, just maybe, he was keeping a secret or two from the world.

As the shock of seeing Colin at her parents' lodge subsided, suspicion bubbled up inside her.

She whirled on her father. "What is this all

about?'' she queried, halfway between annoyance and confusion. "I can't believe you summoned Colin out here, too! For what? Are you and Mom trying to embarrass me? Are you trying to play matchmaker? Not like *that's* going to work.''

"Missy, I have no idea what you're talking about," her father denied gruffly. "And that's no way to greet a guest in our home.''

Holly's jaw dropped and her stomach curled into a knot of astonishment. "Are you telling me you didn't invite him here?''

Her father's eyes narrowed as she took his measure and he returned the favor. After a moment, he firmly shook his head. "No, ma'am.''

Her gaze slid reluctantly to Colin, who confirmed it with a shrug and a grin. "No, ma'am.''

With a gesture indicating she was close to pulling her hair out, she emitted a long, exasperated groan and reached for Colin's free hand, pulling him inside with her and swinging the door closed behind them.

"Welcome to my parents' home," she said smartly, flashing her gaze to her father, who pinched his lips tightly as if annoyed, though his dark, gray-eyed gaze sparkled with amusement.

She turned to Colin, who just smiled at her. She didn't feel like playing games, and Colin wasn't giving her a clue. Her emotions had been jerked around too much today already, thank you very much.

"What are you doing here?" She eyed the worn

backpack he had slung over one shoulder. Clearly he hadn't planned on staying. Long.

But how had he known where to look for her? She gave him another close scrutiny.

His throat was working, but no sound was coming out of his mouth. She decided to help him.

"You were following me?" she suggested, planting her hands on her hips.

Colin didn't know what to make of Holly's audacity. She was clearly upset at someone over something. But he sure didn't know who, or what. This wasn't the way he'd planned his entrance at all.

His gaze slipped unintentionally toward Ian McCade. The man met his gaze head-on, his expression a mixture of welcome and warning.

He wasn't surprised by those sentiments. It hadn't taken long in Holly's father's company to know Ian McCade was going to protect his precious little girl at all costs, and it was a daunting thought.

He swallowed hard. Carrying out this crazy plan to fruition wasn't going to be easy.

He stopped short, wondering for a moment whether he had, once again, dived into the water headfirst without first checking for the depth of the pool. He looked from father to daughter, and thought perhaps there was no water to swim in at all.

He quickly covered the ground he'd tread in his mind, reminding himself of the reason he was here.

Jared Matthews.

When he was searching and praying for an answer to Jared's problem, the solution had come with such ease it had amazed and astonished him.

Jared needed a family. *He* would be Jared's family.

No. *They* would be Jared's family. He and Holly. Together.

In one gigantic flash of insight that was akin, Colin thought, to being hit over the head with a metal beam, clang and all, he had realized the depth of his love for Holly. It was the kind of love a man built the foundation of a family upon.

Not that the idea of loving Holly was such a giant leap for him to make. But the idea of marrying her had popped him *clear* out of the ballpark.

And yet, in that one second he knew marrying Holly was the *right* answer. The *only* answer.

He'd never felt more joy in his life than the moment he'd settled his heart on a life with Holly. And Jared.

He immediately started making plans, starting with a trip up to Holly's parents' lodge to have a man-to-man talk with her father.

It wasn't going to be easy. But he'd known that before he came here.

He just hadn't expected *Holly* to be here. Her visiting here wasn't exactly a typical occasion, from what he knew about this family, and from what Holly had said. She wasn't comfortable here. She didn't exactly come around on a regular basis.

Which meant there was a special occasion of some kind. Or else something was wrong.

He looked from father to daughter, but neither looked grieved, or bereaved, and definitely not overly joyous—only perplexed, and maybe a little annoyed. And curious. Definitely curious.

They wanted to know why he was here. They wanted to know *now*.

And it was a *logical* question, after all.

The only problem was, he didn't have a reasonable answer. At least not one he could share with Holly and her father—yet.

He cleared his throat and prayed God wouldn't look too harshly upon him for this one little fib. "Yes," he said at last, deciding the best course of action was to follow her lead, especially as he was completely unable to come up with a feasible alternative on such short notice. "I...followed you."

Chapter Fourteen

What else could Colin do, except follow Holly's lead and hope he didn't end up in a ditch? He couldn't tell them the real reason he was here, at least not until he'd spoken to her father alone. And he couldn't think of any other sensible reason he'd be at the lodge.

"I—wasn't able to catch you at your apartment, but I was fortunate enough to see you leaving in your Jeep. So I followed you. Uh…here," he added just for good measure.

"Why?" Her hands were still perched on her hips, and her gaze eagle sharp.

He squirmed inwardly, but was careful not to let his thoughts show on his face. What he wanted to do was to blurt everything aloud and get it over with, but he knew better than to let his mouth start flapping right now. He'd insert both his big feet for sure.

If he had any hope at all of winning Holly's heart, never mind her hand in marriage, he had to do it the right way.

Move in slowly. Plan his tactics carefully. Be romantic.

And he should definitely not embarrass her in front of the father she held in such high esteem.

Besides, Ian McCade was the first step in sealing this deal. Ian wouldn't be any happier than Holly would be if Colin asked her to marry him on the spot, without at least giving them a hint of his good intentions beforehand, and leaving a good impression on them both.

Holly audibly cleared her throat. She was still waiting for an answer.

"I'm trying to finish my term paper and I need some help," he said, grimacing at how lame of an excuse he'd concocted.

At first he didn't think Holly bought it, either, but after a moment's hesitation she shrugged and waved him along.

"Come in and sit down. I'll make tuna salad sandwiches for everyone. I can't think about school on an empty stomach." She patted her flat stomach and brushed her palm along the curve of her hip.

Colin's eyes followed her movement and his breath caught and held. She was a beautiful woman in every respect. The man who won her regard was a blessed man, indeed.

He only prayed he would be that man.

He knew he wasn't good enough for her. Holly deserved much better, a more stable man, a man who would wear a watch, who she could count on to be on time for their wedding.

But he was in love with her, and he was enough of an optimist to believe love could conquer all. One thing he knew for certain—he'd gratefully spend his whole life trying to make her happy.

And he would wear a watch for their wedding. The thought brought a grin to his lips.

Glad the invisible hand had finally let go of his chest and allowed him to breathe, he followed Holly into the kitchen. Though the winter morning held a Colorado chill, she was wearing a flowery spring dress that shifted and twirled around her long, sleek legs. He wondered if she'd brought a sweater along, but didn't voice his question aloud, knowing how much Holly valued her independence.

Besides, he hadn't thought to pack any extra clothing at all.

She chatted on about the weather, her Christmas plans and a whole host of other topics, one following closely on top of the other, sometimes with unusual overlaps in thought or subject that made Colin chuckle.

"Are you nervous about something?" he queried, observing that he, himself, was about ready to jump out of his shoes with restlessness.

"No," she denied a bit too quickly. Then she glanced at him and their gazes met and held. Her eyes told him the truth before her lips did. "Yes, I am."

He stroked her arm with the back of his fingers. "What's up?"

She leaned forward until their foreheads nearly touched. "It's my mom and dad," she said in a conspiratorial stage whisper. "I think something's up with them."

Colin lowered his brow. "Why do you say that?" he asked in the same tone of voice she was using.

Holly took his elbow and pulled him into a corner of the kitchen, where she resumed her normal tone of voice. "Well, for one thing, they called me here, but wouldn't tell me why. I asked, but they were vague."

"That does seem a little odd," he agreed. Her parents appeared pretty straightforward to him; not the type to play games, especially with their only daughter.

"As you can probably well imagine, I was terrified at first, because as you can guess, I rarely receive a summons from my parents. For anything."

At least that explained why she was here. "A summons? You sound like you're talking about the Supreme Court. What did they do, send a courier with a missive?"

"Just about. I was sure someone was dying. Why else would they call when it wasn't a holiday?"

"Your dad seems fine."

"His usual gruff self, you mean. Yes, he is. And he assured me my mother is doing well, too. So well, in fact, that she's out shopping right now." She chuckled.

"So if it's not illness, then what?" Colin found his own curiosity growing on the matter.

"When I find out, you'll be the first to know. I must admit it's nice to see a familiar face up here. What's your trouble with your term paper, anyway?" she asked, clearly finished with the subject of her parents, and ready to swim on to bluer water.

Colin's mind froze for a moment, but his slick tongue quickly recovered. "I'm having trouble wrapping my project up for the class. It's such a big idea. I thought you could take a quick look at it for me and see if I'm going in the right direction."

It suddenly occurred to him that he might be asking too much of a woman who was still technically his teacher, at least until the Christmas holiday. He was always bugging her about this thing or that. Her other students weren't haunting her that way.

"Am I putting too much pressure on you?" he asked suddenly. "I mean, you being the professor, me being the student, and all?"

She smothered a laugh with her palm. "And you're asking me now?"

He smacked his hand against his forehead. "I've been taking advantage of the professor all semester long! I'm an idiot."

She shifted so she stood behind him, wrapping her arms around his waist and laying her head against the back of his shoulders. She stood silently for a moment, just holding him.

Colin shuddered with emotion and swallowed hard. He wasn't used to feeling this depth of love, or even of labeling the feelings he was just now recognizing as *love*.

It would take some time getting used to. A lifetime, maybe.

"Do you know that you have been the only stable thing in my life this year?" she asked quietly.

He rumbled with laughter. "Me, stable? That's a scary thought."

She was about to say something in reply when her father entered the kitchen. Holly stiffened as if to move away, but she slowly relaxed her arms and locked her fingers, sealing her arms around his waist. Colin knew it was a big step for her, and he rested his hand lightly on hers for support.

Sergeant McCade narrowed his eyes upon that spot at Colin's waist, and his lips pressed and turned at the corner, one eye half-pinched closed.

Colin held his breath, feeling like a teenager on his first date, not a grown man sharing a close moment with the woman he loved. He could sense that Holly had also stopped breathing.

"Did you want a sandwich, sir?" he offered, holding up the tuna salad sandwich he'd just finished slathering with mayonnaise.

"Sounds good," said Holly's father gruffly. "I was just on my way to the den."

"I'll bring it to you there," Colin said quickly, seizing upon the opportunity he suddenly realized had been presented to him.

Sergeant McCade exited just as quickly as he'd entered, pulling his pipe from his shirt pocket without another word to either of them.

"You're sure you want to do this?" Holly asked as soon as her father was gone, her voice muffled against the denim of Colin's shirt. "I guarantee you're going to get raked over the coals on my account the moment you walk into that room."

"Why would you think that?" He turned in her embrace and put his arms around her. "Just because I happen to have tender feelings toward his daughter?"

She broke the embrace and moved to make another sandwich. "When you put it like that, it doesn't sound so awful."

He wondered why she didn't sound happy about what he'd said. He'd been tentative in his statement, probing her feelings in his own backward way.

Could it be that her emotions did not match his? That she was not in love with him?

No. There was a connection between him. He knew it in his gut.

And if an emotionally impeded student could figure it out, surely a brilliant, stunning professor would have to be in tune with the special bond they shared.

With a forced grin, Holly handed two plates to Colin and gestured toward the den. "It's your skin. Be my guest."

He flashed his most charming grin and gave her a grand wink before heading for the den and the potentially fire-breathing dragon within.

"Sergeant McCade," Colin acknowledged as he entered. "Your sandwich, sir."

The elder man waved him to a seat, and Colin sat uneasily in the blue-patterned Victorian armchair across from the sergeant's easy chair. He sat straight-backed, holding the sandwich awkwardly on his lap.

Ian was already eating, so Colin took a big bite out of the corner of his sandwich. He chewed, but couldn't taste a thing. And the bread must have been too dry, because he was finding it hard to swallow.

He wished desperately he'd thought to bring a bottle of water with him when he'd come in. What good military man made an advance without a good supply of drinking water?

He set his plate aside. He couldn't eat, not when he was literally facing one of the monumental and significant moments he'd ever faced in his life.

Holly's father had no such qualms, and was quietly devouring his sandwich and basically ignoring Colin, which was just as well, as it gave him time to pull

himself together, to pull all his military training together to work for him on this one task.

He only prayed it would sustain him.

"Sir," he said, surprised at how full and even his
voice sounded. Maybe the military had been good for
something after all.

"Brockman."

"May I ask you a question?"

Holly's father gazed at him for a moment, not looking the least bit taken aback that Colin wanted to
speak to him, but with a marked curiosity in his eyes.

Colin held his breath, afraid to so much as swallow
or move a knuckle.

After a moment, the sergeant grunted and nodded
his consent.

Colin had rehearsed the speech a hundred times in
his mind, but now it came out slow and scratchy from
his tight throat and dry mouth. He strained to form
straight, even words, feeling ridiculously awkward.

"I—um—well, I suppose this doesn't come as a
complete shock to you, but I'm in love with your
daughter. I guess I have been for a while now, and
I'm pretty sure that, as her father, you've probably
picked up on those…uh…vibes. Since you know her
so well, I mean."

Sergeant McCade didn't blink an eye.

That being the case, Colin forged on. "Sir, I would
like to ask for your blessing on our marriage."

The sergeant didn't look surprised, or angry, or happy about what Colin had just said.

In fact, it was almost as if Colin hadn't said anything at all.

Slowly, with agonizing patience, Sergeant McCade reached for the pipe sitting on the table beside him. He licked his bottom lip, stoked the pipe carefully and scratched the tip of a wooden match against the bottom of his slipper in order to light the pipe.

He took a puff, then two, closing his eyes to savor the aroma. Finally, after what seemed to Colin like a lifetime, he opened his eyes, tipped his pipe out of the corner of his mouth and cradled it lightly between his thumb and forefinger.

"What does Holly say about all this?"

Colin was so surprised by the question he hardly knew what to say. He'd given this so much thought. He'd thought his battle plan to be foolproof.

He would impress the sergeant by approaching him first, in the traditional, old-fashioned way of doing things.

And then he would have the added ammunition of her father's blessing to take back with him when he went to ask Holly to be his wife.

In the back of his mind, he guessed he had half expected the rugged, commanding sergeant to want to make a decision for Holly on her behalf without her consultation whatsoever.

Not that Colin would have accepted any such thing,

of course, but the thought had been there, that it might happen that way.

Of all the scenarios he'd run in his mind, though, this had definitely *not* been one of them. ''Well, sir, to be honest, I haven't asked her yet.''

He pinched one side of his mouth together over his pipe and said gruffly, ''Don't you think that'd be a good idea?''

Chapter Fifteen

Holly stepped into her parents' stable and inhaled deeply. The combined smell of horse and hay soothed her. It was one of her favorite smells in the whole world.

She'd inherited her mother's love for horses, and she loved to ride, but didn't get much opportunity to be around horses in the city, or even a small university town such as Greeley.

It was only when she was here, at her parents' lodge, that she could shed reality and indulge her childhood fantasies of roping and racing.

This morning, she'd come down to the stable to see her mother's newest asset, a beautiful, shiny black Morgan-cross mare named Belle; but in truth, she'd also escaped the confines of the house to find someplace quiet to think about what her father and mother had revealed to her the previous evening.

Her parents were set on giving her an early inheritance.

They'd told her over dinner. With Colin in the room, like he was family or something.

For some crazy reason, her father had gotten it into his head that he wanted to be around to see her enjoy what money they'd saved up over the years.

It wasn't a fortune, they assured her, but it was enough for her to be able to dream a little bit, and it would be a much needed supplement to her measly salary as a student teacher.

Her father had made a big production of the announcement, telling her over the main course so that she choked on her broccoli and nearly made a scene, dropping her fork with a loud clank onto her plate and standing so suddenly, her chair tipped backward with an additional clatter.

She'd glared at her father, but he'd just pinched the side of his lip and looked satisfied with the way he'd goaded her into a reaction.

Of course, Colin had been there to see the whole debacle. Why her parents had decided Colin ought to be present for such a grand announcement just because he was *there* was beyond her.

And it had been his reaction Holly had dreaded most of all.

He'd merely wiped his mouth with his cloth napkin—Holly thought he did that to hide his amusement, which wasn't very effective, since mirth was shining like a beacon from his eyes—and leaned his elbow on the table, as if he were leaning forward in order to hear better.

Apparently, no one had ever thought to teach Colin it was polite to keep his elbows *off* the table. And though, in her present mood, she'd been inclined to tell him, she was too busy rectifying her own breach in manners.

She didn't know what Colin thought of what her parents had just revealed.

She didn't know what to think.

On one hand, she wanted her parents to spend their money on *themselves* in their retirement. She didn't want any of their hard-earned savings.

Yet her mother had stressed, in her sweet, understated way, what a true desire it would be to give their money to their daughter while they were still living. They wanted to see what a difference they could make in her life.

Being reminded of her mother brought her thoughts back to the present, and Holly moved from stall to stall, looking for the special Morgan mare. As soon as she saw it, she realized what a special find the black was, and Holly immediately fell in love with her.

Picking up a brush and curry comb, she entered Belle's stall. She kept up a steady stream of soft, nonsense talk, and the friendly horse nickered softly in return.

"You're a real beauty," she told Belle. "What beautiful little foals you'll have someday."

Belle shied away from the brush, and Holly laughed. "Oh, don't worry. We don't have any stallions in this stable."

Brushing lightly at her glossy black mane, Holly ran a hand down Belle's sleek neck to calm her, and felt the horse's powerful muscles quiver beneath her touch. "Men can be a handful, can't they, girl?"

Holly sighed inwardly. *Colin* certainly could be labeled a handful.

She still didn't know why he was really here, but she'd bet a year's salary that he wasn't here to work on his term paper. She wouldn't even be surprised if his backpack didn't even contain his books and notes. If she were to hazard a guess, she thought the pack might be toting a spare change of clothes.

Besides, he hadn't even mentioned the need to work on his paper the day before, and he'd had plenty of time to broach the subject with her if that was what was really on his mind.

Which meant he was at her parents' lodge for another reason. And that she could not guess.

Holly had just slipped under Belle's neck to brush her other side when she stopped suddenly to the sound of the stable door opening. The door had squeaked for years, but her father, who did not share his wife's love of horses, had never bothered to oil the hinges.

At first Holly thought to call out to whomever had interrupted her solitude in the stable, but something inside her compelled her to remain silent at the sound of the soft but steady footsteps in the hay.

The unidentified person moved from stall to stall, but did not pause to interact with the horses as Holly would have expected her mother to do. And there was no coarse grumbling that would signify her father's role in the life of the stable—the keeper of the chores.

As the footsteps got nearer, she recognized Colin's low baritone, nickering to the horses and laughing when they responded in kind. He walked to the stall next to Belle's and stopped for a moment.

Holly held her breath.

"Good boy," Holly heard him tell an old paint mare as he reached out to touch her muzzle.

"He's a she," Holly corrected softly, extending her head and arms over the top of the stall door and making Colin take a quick step back, surprise written all over his handsome face.

She laughed with him, both at his rookie mistake, and at the way she'd caught him off guard. "Good *girl* would definitely be a more appropriate moniker. Her name is *Contessa.*"

The paint pushed against Colin's hand, searching in vain for a carrot or a sugar cube, and he patted her neck awkwardly. Evidently they didn't teach equine aptitude in the navy.

"Why don't you try this?" suggested Holly, coming out of Belle's stall and handing Colin a carrot. When he hesitated, she put her hand under his, slowly stroked his own hand open flat, showing him by example the way to feed the mare.

It was an intimate posture, and Holly was intensely aware of the way her arm brushed against his, and the way the rough skin of his knuckles felt under her palm. It was suddenly as if the world had opened up and her senses cascaded to life.

The smell of the freshly thrown hay was transformed into a brisk, delightful aroma. The sound of the horses was like a symphony.

And the sight of the tall, well-built man standing close beside her was like an artist's canvas. His thatch of blond hair blew lightly in the breeze that crept through the cracks in the wood. His face, flushed rosy from the cold, contained a heart-stopping grin. In typical Colin fashion, he hadn't bothered to shave that morning, but to Holly, his adorable, tousled mane and scruff only added to the colossal masculinity he exuded.

She struggled to pull in a breath, and nearly suffocated on the bite of the wintry air. "Keep your hand out straight and she won't mistake your fingers for that carrot," she said with effort.

He looked apprehensive for a moment, but he soon followed her directions, grinning when the old, biddable mare nibbled gently at the carrot, her lips working noisily against the flat of his palm.

"It tickles," he said with a boyish chuckle.

"She's a great little mare," Holly said, stroking the paint's floppy and multicolored forelock. "Contessa was my first horse. She's a smooth ride and a gentle spirit. I think she'll always be my favorite."

Colin was silent, as if absorbing her words. She handed him another carrot and he tentatively moved on to the next stall and Belle, who nickered gladly for the attention.

Holly didn't know what to say, and felt a little like her babbling was breaking up the moment, so she just stood back to enjoy the sight of the charming man become acquainted with her horses.

"So...what brings you out to the stable?" Colin queried lightly, asking the question as if *he* belonged here and *she* was the trespasser.

She gave him a long look before she answered. His gaze gave nothing away. He showed a mild curiosity, nothing more.

"My mother just got a new mare. I came out to see her. Actually, you're feeding her now. This is Belle. She's a Morgan cross."

"I see," said Colin, as if he did. His voice was a good deal lower than usual, and just the tiniest bit gravelly.

"What are *you* doing in the stable?" she blurted, unable to wait one more minute to find out what she'd been wondering all along. "And don't tell me you came out to see the horses, because I won't believe you."

He grinned. "Of course not, Holly. I came out here to see *you.*"

Her heart leapt and started dancing pirouettes in her chest when his warm gaze met hers. Something about the way he was looking at her was *different.* Her heart knew it, as did her lungs, which had suddenly refused to work.

"I'm sorry. Did you need something?" she asked through a clogged throat.

He chuckled. "You could say that."

She leaned her back against the stall door and looked him in the eye. This probably had something to do with his school project, once again.

Bracing herself, she calmed her heart down to below roaring and prepared herself to don the role of teacher, something that was getting more difficult to do where Colin was concerned. "I'm all yours."

Again, he chuckled. "I hope so." This time he sounded nervous.

Colin, *nervous?*

She *must* be imagining things. Colin was many things, but nervous wasn't one of them. She'd never seen him this wound-up before.

He placed his hand on the door above her shoulder and leaned into her, making it more and more difficult for her lungs to discover air to breathe. She inhaled the sweet pungency of soap and man that was the distinctive scent of Colin and thought she might be a little short on oxygen. She was definitely feeling light-headed.

"Were you raised around horses?" he asked, but given the vivid gleam in his eyes, she highly doubted that was the question he wanted to ask.

And she was having trouble forming an answer. The words were in her mind, but there seemed to be an electrical short in the link between her brain and her tongue.

"No," she croaked out at last. "Not as a child, anyway. Horses have always been my mother's dream, but because of the military lifestyle, we moved around too much to own horses."

He leaned closer. "I'm glad she finally had the opportunity to fulfill her dreams. When *did* she get her first horse?"

Again, Holly had the distinct feeling he was postponing the moment when he'd blurt out what he really wanted to say.

"When she was forty-seven years old, although if you tell her I even remotely alluded to her age, she won't talk to me for a week."

"My lips are sealed," he promised in a whisper, marking a silent *x* across his mouth with the tip of his finger.

Holly smiled gently, both at Colin and at the memory of her mother. "She often tells me her life started when she got her first horse. Except for having me, of course. Though she always adds that part as an afterthought,'' she said with an edgy chuckle.

She wished she was able to retreat from the feel of his breath on her cheek, and his arms so close about her but not quite touching her. But the stable door didn't give way under the force of her prayer, however fervently made. And it held strong behind her back.

''What are you really doing out here, Colin?'' she asked abruptly, deciding to force his hand while she grappled for the stable door handle.

''I want to marry you.''

His words, though softly uttered, hit her with the force of a navy torpedo.

What could he be saying to her? She hadn't the slightest idea why he wanted to see her when she'd asked him about his motive in visiting the stable, but a marriage proposal had been about as far from her mind as the earth from the moon.

Marriage. They hadn't even talked around the word, much less seriously worked through the many aspects of their relationship. She wasn't even sure they *had* a relationship.

She pulled in a breath and held it, waiting for time and reality to smooth out her world. She looked back at Colin, focused on his smiling, expectant face, and the plain leveled.

It was *Colin* asking that ridiculous and completely

unexpected question. Slowly her heart resumed beating again.

With effort, she laughed and nodded in understanding. It was his idea of a joke, but he'd caught her off guard. "Right. Now tell me what you really want."

To her surprise, *he* looked surprised. Genuinely astonished.

"No, Holly. I really mean what I'm saying. I want to marry you."

"Colin," she warned, trying to keep her voice from shaking.

He was being mean, playing a spiteful joke, whether he realized it or not. It wasn't like him to be insensitive, especially on purpose.

"Holly, how can I convince you I'm in earnest here?" he asked, his voice low and fervent. Determination glimmered from his eyes. "No, wait. I know what will do the trick."

He rummaged through his fleece-lined jean jacket pocket with his free hand. "Will this convince you I mean what I say?"

Holly swept in a breath. Colin flipped open the top of a small, black velvet box to reveal an engagement ring. A lovely solitaire sparkled brightly even in the dim light of the stable.

"I...don't understand," she whispered hoarsely, clenching her hands together in front of her.

His smile wavered for a moment, but soon his confident grin reemerged. He lifted the diamond toward her, as if somehow she hadn't seen it.

She wasn't blind. Only struck dumb by the irony of the eternal bachelor asking *her* to be his wife.

"It would be great if we could be married as soon as possible," he said, grasping her left hand in his right and rubbing her ring finger with his thumb.

Holly's heart was roaring in her head. All her feelings for Colin rose up to greet her, and she was astonished at the intensity of the love she felt.

How had she not realized this before?

She was in love with Colin Brockman.

Deciding the answer to his question—even if he hadn't quite *asked* the actual question—was one of the easiest things she'd done in all of her life.

Of course she'd marry him.

Or at least she thought she would. Until the next words out of his mouth changed *everything*.

"I've got to adopt Jared Matthews soon, or he'll be sent off to foster care again and I'll lose my window of opportunity."

"What?"

"It will be much easier to convince a judge I'm worthy as a married man. And of course I was happy to hear about your early inheritance," he continued as if she had not frozen in his arms, her jaw dropped in astonishment. "The extra money is going to be like a windfall to mention at the hearing."

The affirmation poised on her lips died a sudden,

painful death. The reality of the truth washed through her in wave after nauseating wave.

Colin didn't *love* her.

He didn't really want to be married in the first place. He was doing this for the sake of a *kid*.

She squeezed her eyes closed, as the stain of her own sinfulness crept up to mock her, sneaking into her thoughts again though she thought she'd put the past long behind her.

She reminded herself quickly that God had washed her white as snow. She'd started fresh.

Besides, the rejection she was feeling now had nothing to do with what she'd done in the past, because Colin didn't even know the way she'd lived as a teenager.

But knowing that didn't stop her from embracing the feeling she wasn't good enough for a man like Colin. She couldn't help it. Years of poor self-esteem had set her up for this moment.

The pain of rejection raged through her despite all her inward protests. It seemed ridiculous to feel unwanted when she was being proposed to, but no matter how she tried to look at it, she couldn't break free of the sting of her conclusions.

It was obvious he was essentially settling on second best, asking her to marry him because she was his friend, and the most obvious choice given his present set of circumstances.

He'd do anything he had to do to take care of Jared

Matthews, up to and including marrying a decent, convenient woman.

And she was that convenient woman. Money and everything.

She didn't know how she could bear the heart-wrenching pain in her chest; nor did she quite know how she would retain her dignity in the moment. She only knew she must, and she would—somehow.

Perhaps the answer lay with the word *decent*. Colin needed a virtuous and godly woman to raise his adopted son. He was looking to her because he didn't know better.

Well, he was going to know better now. He was going to know the truth. And then he would do what any good, upstanding man looking for a mother for his child would do—get out of Dodge.

"Colin, there is a lot you don't know about me," Holly began, raising her chin and meeting his gaze head-on.

"Of course, sweetheart. I know I'm rushing things, but you know I've got a good reason. And we'll have plenty of time to learn all the ins and outs once we're married, don't you think?"

Holly wanted to groan. He was so naive, it was almost scary. She wouldn't believe he was for real, if she hadn't been around him long enough to know he was the genuine article.

"I think you need to know about me now."

Colin leaned forward, so his breath was brushing her cheek. "Okay. So tell me."

She couldn't think when he acted that way. She shoved him backward with both palms. "You can't marry me, Colin. After what I'm about to tell you, you won't even want to marry me."

"There's nothing you can tell me that will make me change my mind," he vowed.

She laughed without mirth. "Believe me, I've heard that before. No man wants what I have to offer. At least no Christian man."

"And what's that, Holly? What's so bad that I'm going to run screaming from the stable?" He sounded as if he was getting angry now. That was just as well, Holly thought. Better anger than hate, or worse, revulsion.

"Let's just say I wasn't a saint in high school," she said, not knowing how to say what needed to be said, and desperate to have it out and over with. "I didn't become a Christian until college. I drank beer. I smoked cigarettes. I partied with a wild crowd."

"And?"

He was going to make her say it.

She looked away. "I'm not a virgin, Colin. Not even close."

With a muffled sob, she ducked under his arm and ran away, as fast and as far as her legs would carry her. Away from Colin, and any future they might have had.

Chapter Sixteen

Colin didn't know what kind of reaction he ought to expect from Holly after his sudden marriage proposal, but dropping what she must have thought was a bomb on him and then running frantically from the quiet stable wasn't even on the list.

Neither was having her Marine Corps drill sergeant father come raging down on him like a dog on a T-bone steak.

Teeth bared and everything.

That man definitely did *not* like to see his only daughter upset. It was a wonder Colin escaped with his skin, never mind his sanity.

Well, that wasn't quite true. While his skin was still intact, his sanity was questionable.

He hadn't been the same since he'd returned to the unaltered silence of his apartment, the sparkling new diamond ring meant for Holly buried deep in the pocket of his fleece-lined jean jacket.

He'd come home weighing a great deal less than when he'd left. There was an immense, gaping empty space where his heart had once resided.

He slumped onto the couch, groaning half in welcome, half in misery. Rascally Scamp pattered onto his lap and pawed at his stubbly chin for attention.

His kitten was right. Colin knew he looked like a wreck, his green plaid shirt half-untucked from his jeans, and his hair looking as if he'd been raking his fingers through it all day.

He *had* been messing with his hair. Not so much because it was troublesome so much as the fact that he was busting out of his bones, going out of his mind over the way things had worked out. He felt every bit as miserable as he looked.

"Whaddaya think, Scamp, ol' fellow? Did I blow it big time, or what?"

Scamp only purred in response, arranging the untucked side of Colin's shirt into a nice little kitty bed with his paw, and comfortably settling himself upon it with a contented *mew*.

"I wish I was a cat," Colin said grumpily.

Scamp licked his paw clean and swiped it over his fluffy black-and-white ear, the self-proclaimed king of the castle. Colin, on the other hand, felt like a pawn in a game a good deal larger than he was.

Where had he gone wrong?

With what he hoped was a critical eye, he reviewed the series of events that had led up to Holly's stark rejection of his proposal.

He frowned, finding it hard to concentrate. He'd been feeling unusually emotional lately. Ever since he'd met Holly, in fact.

But definitely more so this weekend. He wasn't sure he could trust himself to be rational.

Especially now.

Proposing to Holly had seemed like such a good idea at the time. He, who'd sworn off children as if he were allergic to them, had become father material the moment he'd heard of Jared's dilemma and realized he could provide a stable home where others could or would not.

The next logical progression in his chain of thought was to consider getting married, to improve his chances to adopt the boy and to provide Jared with a stable home with a father *and* a mother.

So he was a little slow on the take. It was only then that he'd realized he *wanted* to get married—to Holly—and not because of Jared, though adopting the little boy made the deal even sweeter in his mind.

Holly McCade was the right woman for him, the woman he wanted to spend the rest of his life with. It had only taken a catastrophe to goad his brain into figuring out what his heart already knew.

Holly as his wife, and Jared as his son. Holly Brockman. Jared Brockman.

Until then he hadn't put a word to his feelings for Holly.

Love.

He wanted to hoot and holler and scream and cry, all at once. His feelings were at once so incredibly simple, and so largely complicated, that it went beyond description.

He was in love with her.

And she, he decided, thoughtfully and carefully, was in love with him. She'd been the sensitive, expressive one in their relationship, and he'd been the big dolt who hadn't known enough to grab on to a good woman when he had the chance. She'd hinted again and again of her feelings in a look, a touch. Even the special meaning she placed upon their kisses should have clued him in.

But he was hopelessly dull in the romance department, and he'd never let on how he felt about her. How could he, when he hadn't known himself?

He'd decided to fix that omission as soon as possible. His heart was in the right place. All that had been left for him to do was to buy a pretty diamond ring and ask Holly to become his wife.

Unfortunately, the actual event hadn't been nearly as uncomplicated as his daydream.

At first, it appeared she hadn't understood the question. Which was highly preferable to what happened when she *did* figure out what he was saying.

She'd been so distressed. Her cheeks had turned an

alarming shade of pink, her breath had come in tight gasps and her voice was shrill. She hadn't returned the sentiment he had offered.

Instead, she'd thrown her past in his face. Reminded him of how difficult and different her life had been like before she had found a Savior.

It broke his heart to think of what she must have been through. She'd suffered much. But why bring it up now? Did she think he hadn't been through enough in his own miserable life to be able to commiserate?

There must have been something—something he'd said or done to make her run away from him the way she did. Somehow, he had the gut feeling he was responsible for how their relationship now lay in ruins.

The question was, how was he going to straighten out this big mess?

He didn't have time to ponder the answer to that question because the telephone rang.

Holly!

He rummaged frantically through the basket of unfolded clean clothes he'd left on the floor by the fireplace, sure the ring was coming from somewhere in that vicinity.

It took him three rings to find the receiver and juggle it to his ear, but he answered with a full-toothed grin.

"Holly?"

"Mr. Brockman, this is Michelle Walker at Marston House."

Colin's hopes fell into his gut like a lead cannonball. He recovered slowly. "Hi, Michelle. How's Jared?"

"Holding his own," Michelle answered promptly. "Greatly due to your assistance."

"I can't take credit for that," Colin denied with a grimace. "God's the one taking care of that terrific little boy."

"Yes, well, let us hope so. Jared is the reason I'm calling."

Colin's gut clenched, and he grit his teeth. "Go ahead."

"I've spoken to social services on your behalf. They are willing to hold a hearing on your proposition, first for Jared's placement, and then for his permanent adoption into your household."

Colin squeezed his eyes closed, as close as he'd ever been to shedding tears. This would have been good news, if only...

"I hear a *but* coming," he said wryly, his throat closed and his voice scratchy with emotion.

Michelle gave a nervous chuckle. "Smart man. Here's the thing. Before you can get that hearing, you have to meet with a team of psychologists appointed by the state. It's a five-member panel of men and women from this area who'll be, basically, judging your suitability as a father for Jared."

His suitability as a father.

Colin felt as if he'd had his legs cut out from under him. Five minutes ago, he'd thought himself about as low as he could possibly go.

Now he knew it could be worse.

He had no illusions about his chances to have Jared as his son. As a single man, it would take a miracle for a judge to even consider giving him custody of the young, troubled boy.

And that was when he had only two hearings to contend with.

But now he was looking at standing a minimum of three times up before a judge or panel, and he found he didn't quite believe in miracles anymore.

He silently reached for heavenly support, but his faith was wavering under the strain, and God's comfort seemed far away.

"Don't worry too much about it, Colin," Michelle added when he didn't answer her right away. "These are all going to be friends and colleagues of Holly. I'm sure you'll do fine."

Fine? He clenched his fists and set his jaw against the anger and torrid feelings of helplessness raging through him.

Hadn't he been questioning himself these past couple of weeks? He'd run headlong into the idea of adopting Jared because he knew in his gut in was the right thing for him to do. And because he wanted to do it.

But when the pragmatic side of him sat down and looked at it, there was a great deal more to the story than that. As long as he'd held out hope that Holly would be in the picture, at least he had her loving kindness to fall back on.

Now he only had himself. And he wasn't sure if he could do it. There were moments when he wasn't sure he wanted to do it, wasn't sure what adopting the boy would mean for his career, and now—without Holly—for the rest of his life. Alone.

Jared had special needs. Could he handle it? Could he father the boy and still attend college and seminary full-time? What about the navy after that? What about the moving around?

Could he offer Jared the stability he needed, without Holly there to help?

Colin squared his jaw and his shoulders. Of course he could. He would make it work, just as he'd worked out all the other challenges he'd faced in his life. He would do what was right, and deal with the consequences as they occurred.

Hadn't Jesus Himself said to take it one day at a time?

Slowly, his mental, physical and spiritual strength returned, and with it, his resolve to do what was in his heart. He had to try, for Jared's sake. But could it possibly get any worse?

He cringed. Somehow, he thought if it were possible, it would probably get worse. He'd never been a pessimist. But he'd never felt more alone in the world than he did at that moment.

It had been two weeks, and Holly still hadn't recovered enough to resume her normal activities, including teaching her classes at the university. She'd told Sarah she was sick—and she was.

Sick at heart.

Her parents had been surprisingly gracious, allowing her to stay at the lodge and mope around as long as she wanted. Her mother brought her dinner in her room when she didn't show up for a meal; and to her surprise, her gruff old father didn't say a single word about Colin's misspoken and untimely proposal, not even to say *I told you so,* though she was certain the sergeant knew all about what had happened.

That no one spoke of the matter hadn't kept her from thinking about it, of course. In fact, Colin was about all she thought about, locked in her room with the curtains drawn and the television humming. Every look, every smile, every shared kiss replayed in her mind, a brand of self-torture she hadn't realized she was capable of.

When she returned home to her apartment, it was with a new mind. She let herself grieve for the broken relationship, and though she hadn't been able to sweep Colin completely from her mind, she knew it was time to move on with her life.

And the beginning of any new life, she knew, was

a clean house. She started by opening the blue ging-ham curtains wide to reveal the sunlight. She swept and mopped and vacuumed until every room in her studio apartment was spotless and sparkling.

She prayed, soul searched and found something she didn't realize she had.

Self-respect. And strength. For the first time she had to confront her past within her present reality, and though she thought it might be counted a loss, she decided to count it a win.

She was still standing.

She was ready to make a go of it. She was anxious to get back to teaching. And she was ready to start her career in social services, as well. If she'd learned one lesson from all this, it was that there was very little black-and-white in the world.

She wanted to fight on the side of the good, make whatever little dent in the world she could make.

And still there was Colin.

Because she wanted to understand, to move on, she returned to the iniquitous moment in her mind, the replay painful but necessary. She knew the words by heart, remembered every movement, every expres-sion.

He'd never even really asked her to marry him, technically, and she wondered if he even knew. And yet, for all that, it *was* a marriage proposal, one with strings attached.

How could Colin, her sweet, sensitive Colin, have

treated her with such arrogance, such mockery? After all the time and experiences they'd shared together, she'd thought Colin was her friend—in truth, her best friend, the best friend she'd ever had.

And more, she knew she loved him, though she'd never told a living soul of her feelings. She hadn't been certain of her own heart herself until Colin had mentioned marriage.

Had it only been her imagination, thinking he might reciprocate those feelings?

One would think it to have been a possibility, considering he'd proposed to her. His part of the bargain would have been to have and to hold, as well.

But maybe he wasn't taking into account his own feelings. He'd certainly acted as if her acceptance of his marriage proposal was a given, a done deal before it even started, with no regard to *her* feelings whatsoever.

As if there were no question that she would immediately fall into his arms, or at least agree to wear his ring. As if the courtesy of asking didn't matter. As if her strength and dignity could withstand his callous behavior.

How little he really knew her.

Did he *really* think she would enter into a loveless marriage with him, even for the sake of a sweet little boy like Jared Matthews?

Did he really think love didn't matter?

What kind of a wife could she be to Colin without

love? What kind of mother would she be to poor Jared Matthews?

The question echoed through her head, stunning her heart back to life. What kind of mother, indeed?

Tossing the mop aside, she cranked up the stereo with some classic rock music, took a long-armed lamb's wool duster and began dusting the ceiling fans and the tops of the doorways.

Her thoughts turned to the little autistic boy who'd won Colin's affection, as well as hers, over the last few months, and she felt a flash of guilt.

What would happen to the little boy if she and Colin weren't there for him?

She didn't know when Jared had stopped being just one of many kids, and had become a personal issue, but that's how she thought of him now. As her own personal problem. The way Colin obviously thought of Jared, too.

When she'd run away from Colin that day in the barn, she'd been thinking of herself—first, and only. She'd been feeling so sorry for herself she hadn't given a thought to the plight of that little boy.

Perhaps it was to Colin's credit that he was so set on making this small, but critical, difference in the world. Perhaps she was looking at this whole set of circumstances through the wrong set of lenses. Maybe Colin had never meant to hurt her at all.

He *had* hurt her with his assumptions, but she now

acknowledged that it was possible he'd had other things on his mind that day. Noble things.

Like Jared.

Of course, when it came to marriage and a lifetime together, *she* wanted to be the first one on his mind and in his heart, after God. But a precious little boy in distress wasn't a bad runner-up.

It was saying something that Colin was willing to give up his freedom in order to save Jared. She knew how much he valued liberty. Freedom to go and do as he liked was paramount to the man. Hadn't he rebelled against anything remotely stifling and autocratic—even a wristwatch?

He'd always shied away from the idea of marriage, never mind children. He was afraid he was going to turn out like his father.

And suddenly he wanted to take on both a wife and a son?

Michelle Walker had let her know that Colin was going up before a jury of her peers, in order to determine whether a preliminary custody hearing was in order. And while she knew Colin would pass the tests of charm and integrity with flying colors, without her help, he could not produce a wife.

He could not provide the secure, white-picket-fence kind of household Holly knew the board would be looking for. He couldn't show the stability he'd never known and was desperately grasping for.

The truth was there before her, and she knew it.

Colin no doubt knew it, too. And it was no doubt breaking his heart.

No single man, no matter how persuasive and sincere, would hazard a chance of adopting a special-needs child like Jared Matthews. Her heart fell for the future of the little boy. And, to her surprise, her heart fell for Colin's future, too.

As suddenly as those emotions overwhelmed her, she knew there was another way.

She could help. She wanted to make a difference in the world.

She could. She could make *all* the difference in the life of one little boy, and Lord willing, in the life of the man she loved.

Even if he didn't return those sentiments.

It was a crazy idea. Yet once the thought had crossed her mind, she couldn't get rid of it. It nagged at her, buzzing around her mind like a gnat.

What if she agreed to marry Colin?

Was it possible God could work through the situation on Jared's behalf? Was it possible Colin might come to love her over time?

In taking care of Jared, she could use all the skills she'd spent a lifetime building. She'd always wanted to do something really special, really meaningful with her life's work. Working with Jared would fit right in with her career in social work.

And old-fashioned as it was, it appealed to her to make a home for Colin and Jared. She thought she might find great joy and fulfillment taking care of her husband and children, at least if her childhood daydreams were anything to go by.

She could build a place where love and laughter spread as much warmth as a fire in the hearth. She could make a place that Colin would look forward to coming home to, and that would give Jared the sense of safety and routine he needed to thrive. And they already had a kitten.

The dream broke through like a waterfall.

Did love conquer all?

Her past rose up to greet her, taunting her, reminding her just how far from *love* she had once drifted. Ironic, how a teenage girl gave up her virtue and her morals looking to be loved.

Really loved.

It wasn't until she'd found God's love that human love, especially between men and women, began to make any sense. Clothed in the mantle of God's love, she was finally able to recognize her own capacity to give love, and hopefully, eventually, to receive love.

A Scripture she'd learned in childhood rose up to greet her like the morning sun. She remembered it word for word, the verse chiming out in her old Sunday school teacher's bell-tone voice, clearly enunciated and ringing with clarity.

Closing her eyes, she smiled at God's wisdom.

There is faith, hope and love. But the greatest of these is love.

It could work. It could really work!

Chapter Seventeen

Colin was sweating. He was *really* sweating, not just politely perspiring. And he knew the droplets forming against his temple and dripping onto his eyebrows weren't helping him look his very best before the five-member psychological panel.

Sweating, whether from stress, or maybe from downright fear, was not the impression he wanted to leave with the state board that held his life—and little Jared's—in his hands.

Trying not to make a big show of it, he pulled a carefully ironed handkerchief from the back pocket of his pants and swiped it surreptitiously across his damp brow and across his freshly shaved upper lip.

He quickly shoved the cloth back into his pocket when the dour-faced, gray-haired woman sitting at the end of the five-person panel—a woman Colin stopped just short of classifying as an old broad, out of kindness, not of truth—caught his attention and sent bolts of alarm through him.

Staring at him coldly, she tapped her pencil against the table in an erratic beat that hammered in a merciless, burning rhythm in Colin's brain that made him want to grab his head and run.

This from a man who didn't *get* headaches. But this was a special occasion, and the throbbing in his head matched the painful throbbing in his heart.

Ms. Dour Face stared at him without saying a word. He met her gaze straight on, letting her know in his own quiet way that he had nothing to hide.

She, on the other hand, was giving nothing away. If only someone on the panel would smile at him, give him some hope or encouragement that they were really considering his request, and not just paying lip service to it.

That he wasn't here on a lost cause.

His worst fear was that they'd made their judgment before he'd even had a chance to speak his case. They'd asked a few preliminary questions, but hadn't let him launch into the soliloquy he'd prepared on Jared's behalf, the one where he listed all the reasons he would make a good father.

With what he had going against him, it wasn't beyond the possibility that they'd sealed his fate without listening to a word he might have to say on his own behalf, or on behalf of little Jared.

He reminded himself that these were Holly's friends and colleagues, but somehow, that only made him feel more alone. What he wouldn't give for Holly by his side right now. He, the king of independence, finally admitting it would be nice to have a woman's hand to hold.

No one had ever accused him of being good on his timing.

The board stirred, looking at their watches and then at each other, whispering guardedly behind file folders held up to block their faces from his view. Colin swallowed hard and resisted the urge to once again swipe at his beaded forehead.

"Mr. Brockman, can you tell the board how you originally came into contact with Jared Matthews?" A pretty young blonde on the panel asked that question.

Happy to have the opportunity to speak, Colin launched into the story of meeting Jared as part of the school project. The board clearly recognized and acknowledged Holly's name and role in this. Colin hoped she wouldn't mind that he'd mentioned her part.

At the board's insistence, he continued with how he'd returned to Marston House and befriended the boy, and then was there for him during various crises the boy had experienced.

"We have testimonials from Marston House on your behalf," the man in charge assured him.

Colin cleared his throat. "You do?"

"Yes, sir. It seems you have worked some miracles with Jared."

He grinned. "Yes, sir. Well, God's in the miracle-working business, but I'm always glad to help."

"Tell us truly," said the dour-faced woman, "why you would want to adopt a boy with autism."

He looked her straight in the face. He looked them all straight in the face. "Because I love him."

It was so quiet in the room, there wasn't a single paper rattling. "That's a good answer," said the pretty blond woman.

The board stopped and conferred with one another behind their files.

They were close to a decision.

Colin's heart was in his throat. When the leader of the board, Trey Adams, stood and nodded to him, he stood, as well—shoulders squared, feet planted and his head held high.

"Mr. Brockman," Trey began, then cleared his throat and looked for support to the four ladies that completed his panel.

Colin didn't like that pause, or the way Trey Adams pursed his lips.

"Let me start out by saying I've never met a man with your personal concern for a child not his own, particularly a young man with special needs.

"In my experience, most men don't take an active interest in social work, and certainly not to the point to which you've extended yourself by being here today. We are all very impressed, and you are to be highly commended.''

Colin pinched his lips into a semblance of a grin and nodded his head. He could feel a *but* coming, and he knew before the words were spoken that it was going to be one big *nevertheless*.

''You must know that you more than qualify in most of the areas we were looking at today,'' Trey went on, a little less tentative than a moment before. He steepled his fingers and stroked the bottom of his thick black goatee. ''We are concerned, however, that you lack one crucial quality, a characteristic that makes us more than a little hesitant to recommend you.''

Colin stood rigidly, military stiff, and braced himself for the unwelcome news.

Trey paused a moment, cleared his throat and continued. ''While your integrity and love for Jared are evident and highly commendable, and while you've shown yourself to be a good physical provider with a fine future ahead of you, it concerns us nevertheless that you are an unmarried man.''

There it was, out on the table.

Colin fingered the collar of his dress whites. He'd wanted to create a presence with his uniform, but instead it felt confining, wrapping around him like a straitjacket and strangling him like a noose.

Finally, the matter had been voiced. It was out in

the open for everyone to see. Now, if they'd only let him openly address the issue, he might be able to persuade them what a good parent he would be.

He had barely lifted his head to begin his first argument when he was stopped in his tracks by a voice from the back of the room, a rich, warm voice he knew as well as his own.

"Oh, but, Trey, you're mistaken," Holly announced, pausing to catch her breath as she entered the room. She'd obviously been running. Her face was prettily flushed and she was obviously struggling to pull in air, one hand propped on her hip, and the other bracing her knee, as if she'd run a marathon.

"What's this about, Holly?" Trey asked, sounding as baffled as Colin felt. "I think I speak for the rest of us here when I say I'm a little confused."

Holly pulled herself upright and marched to Colin's side, her sleek black attaché bouncing on her hip and her high-heeled shoes clicking with every step. She slid an arm through his as if it was the most natural thing in the world, and smiled up at him with a brand of encouragement that left Colin's heart racing and his head reeling.

She'd never looked better.

She turned to the panel with a confident, poised smile. "Trey. Panel members." She nodded to each one, addressing them as if she were the lawyer pleading his case. And indeed, that was what she seemed to be, especially when she spoke her next words.

"Colin and I have decided to step up our wedding plans the tiniest bit so we can take care of little Jared *together* at the earliest opportunity."

The word *together* reverberated through the room, echoing off the walls, bouncing from the window wells and ringing through Colin's ears.

Marriage? What marriage was she talking about? Last information he had, they weren't even on speaking terms, much less conjugal ones.

He slid her a look he hoped she'd read accurately. He wanted to know the truth now, before things got any deeper in the mud!

She refused to look at him straight on, instead choosing to address the panel once more. "Colin and I were going to get married eventually, so moving forward the date makes sense for all of us. Jared will have a real mother and father who love him and are completely committed to him from the first day he comes home to live with us."

She paused, making eye contact with every person in the room except Colin. "Colin and I agree that we want to give Jared a permanent, stable home. As you know, I'm a licensed psychologist, and Colin is currently in seminary to take orders to be a navy chaplain. I assure you that you won't find better parents than Colin and me for that little boy.

"What's more, Jared Matthews isn't just any little boy. We've both spent extra time with him, and we've both grown to love him very much. Each of us has faith in God that Jared can and should be a member of the home we are building.''

She pulled tightly but surreptitiously on Colin's arm, nudging him closer to her. He noticed that she was gritting her teeth even as she was smiling, but he put on a good face for the panel, taking a kind of backward joy in the opportunity to wrap his arm around the woman he loved and planting a healthy, smacking kiss on her lips.

''My fiancée,'' he announced, smugly eyeing the panel of Holly's peers. ''She'll make an excellent mother for Jared, don't you think?''

Trey made a surprised sound in the back of his throat and sat down. Again, papers and files surreptitiously covered faces as the panel whispered and deliberated amongst themselves.

Colin stared down at Holly, unable to find his voice through the emotion clouding his throat, but desperately wanting to know what was going on inside that pretty head of hers.

She still wouldn't look at him. Her fingers, gripping tightly around his waist, tapped an erratic rhythm, and Colin could only guess at her nervousness at being here.

His own gut was still tight with anxiety over the situation.

But now, for the first time, there was the real likelihood—the real *hope*—he might have a go at raising Jared.

Thanks to Holly.

Trey smiled as the panel grew quiet. "We want to offer our congratulations," he said, his gaze moving from Colin to Holly, and back again.

"Thanks, Trey," Holly said smoothly, covertly yanking on the back of Colin's uniform jacket to bring him up to speed. Colin couldn't think of what to do besides smile and nod, and let Holly do the talking. She was obviously good at it.

"We think you make a fantastic couple," Trey continued. "And we think you'll make equally fantastic parents to Jared Matthews."

Colin felt a rush of triumph at the words, but not for himself. For his future wife and son! He beamed down at Holly, his angel of mercy.

He offered a silent prayer thanking God for the privilege of being able to love a woman like Holly, and the opportunity to raise Jared Matthews. He knew he'd never be able to make it up to Holly for the sacrifice she'd made today, but one thing he knew for certain—he'd spend his whole life trying.

Colin was only glad Holly had finally come to recognize that she loved him, and that she was showing her commitment to him in a tangible way with her dedication to Jared. No one had to tell him that there weren't very many women in the world willing to make those kinds of sacrifices in the name of love.

Holly, though her face was bright with their mutual success, refused to look him straight in the eye.

After a moment, she placed her knuckles against the table and grinned up at Trey and the board. "We do appreciate your confidence."

"We'll recommend your case be heard as soon as you sign the marriage license," Trey assured them both with a wide smile as he presented them with a variety of legal documents to sign. "Of course, this is only the first step, but we have confidence that you two are going to go the distance. Just let us know what your plans are, and we'll act accordingly."

He'd know, all right, Colin thought. The whole *world* would know when he made Holly his wife. They'd be able to hear him shouting a million miles away.

Nearly shaking with happiness and wondering how he'd ever lived without the emotions he was now experiencing, he took Holly by the elbow and escorted her briskly from the room. He wasn't about to give the panel any time to reconsider their assessment.

"Jared thanks you, and I thank you," he said, planting a juicy kiss on her cheek the moment they were outside.

He'd rushed her out the door, eager to take her in his arms, share the depth of his joy with her and properly kiss the woman who would soon become his wife.

But something in her eyes stopped him. Something was not quite right.

While she looked as radiant as he'd ever seen her,

with her cheeks becomingly flushed and her sable hair glistening with red highlights in the winter sunshine, her eyes did not glow with the same intensity he expected of her.

With the same intensity he felt.

Her smile faltered and wavered, and then disappeared altogether. "There are some conditions," she said, her voice cool and collected. Too calm.

"I beg your pardon?" he asked coarsely, wondering how, in his happy delirium, he'd missed the part about the *conditions* of pursuing custody of Jared. Had it been part of the written paperwork they'd signed?

Was it something to do with their marriage? Did he need to purchase a home or jump through some hoop before they could really be a family?

Whatever it was, it would happen. He was determined to see to that.

"I agree to become a military wife," she began, finally looking him in the eye. She looked determined, but not particularly happy.

It wasn't what he expected at all, and definitely not what he wanted. He hadn't expected her to show up today. But when she had—well, he'd at least thought she'd be happy about it.

"I agree," she repeated. "But you, in turn, must let me take care of the children."

Colin felt like he'd been hit in the head with a

sledgehammer. This wasn't about the panel, or even about adopting Jared.

He opened his mouth to ask what was really going on, but she held up a hand and cut him short.

"That's right, I said *children*. If we're going to be married, and apparently we are, it is going to be a real marriage, in every regard. A two-way street, with respect on both sides of the fence."

She paused, but he could tell she wasn't finished, so he didn't try to speak.

"I also want a real wedding. I refuse to run away and elope with you."

"Holly, I never said I wanted—"

"My parents won't settle for any less than the works. Dress. Flowers. Cake."

Visions of wedding works danced in Colin's head, and he swallowed hard. While he'd never actually considered eloping with her, he did have to admit the many details of planning an actual *wedding* had escaped him.

She swept in a breath and delivered her ultimatum with a grand gesture of her arm. "And I want children of our own someday."

Colin frowned, perplexed. Of course she wanted children of her own. She was going to make the world's best mother. There was no argument there. "Holly, I think you—"

Again, she cut him off. "I'm perfectly content with my decision, Colin," she assured him. But somehow that declaration only made him feel more ill at ease with the situation.

"You just caught me off guard, the first time. That's all."

Colin pressed his lips together and took a good look at the woman he was preparing to marry. Perhaps that was what was wrong—that he'd somehow botched the marriage proposal, dashing out to ask her to be his wife without first preparing her for the surprise.

But somehow, he thought it was more.

He *knew* it was more.

Maybe it had something to do with what she was trying to tell him that day in the stable. All that stuff about her past, her life before she became a Christian.

Whatever it was, he had to know.

He took her by the shoulders and locked his gaze with hers, not allowing her to turn away this time. He was a man determined to get answers. "Holly, I want you to take a deep breath."

She complied with an audible sigh.

"Okay, then. Now I want you to tell me what in the world you are talking about!"

Chapter Eighteen

Colin stopped fidgeting the moment he donned his white, navy dress uniform, but his heart was still wiggling around in his chest like a two-year-old on a hard church pew. With effort, he steeled his nerves and faced the mirror, attempting to make final adjustments to his tight collar.

"How do I look, buddy?" he asked Jared Matthews, who was sitting at a table in the corner of a room, assembling a puzzle.

Jared, adorable in a black tuxedo, looked up at Colin and strained to focus his gaze. "Colin...is... good," he pronounced slowly.

Colin laughed. "Wow, pal, I hope Holly thinks so, too. I can't believe how nervous I am."

"H-o-lll-eeeee," Jared agreed happily, before returning his attention to the puzzle.

Suddenly it sounded as if someone was trying to bulldoze the door down, and Colin whirled hastily, his clammy palm slipping against the door handle as he tried to turn the knob.

Ian McCade marched in, looking smart and intimidating in his Marine Corps dress uniform, his shoes spit-polished and his seams straight and even.

The sergeant didn't mince words. He strode to Colin and faced him down—or up, as the case happened to be, since Colin was four inches taller than his future father-in-law.

Colin was almost annoyed by the habitual way his own military training took over. Without a bit of conscious thought, he squared his shoulders, stood an inch taller and tipped his chin up, staring straight forward instead of directly into Sergeant McCade's eyes, which would have been a sign of disrespect.

"Are you ready to get married?" Ian barked into his face.

"What?" What else would he be here for, all decked out in his dress whites and getting ready within moments to proceed into the McCades' great room and stand at the end of an aisle, where wedding bells were ringing?

What was the man trying to insinuate?

In moments, he would gladly join his hand and his heart with Holly forever, giving her his name and his home in addition to his life.

"You hard of hearing, boy?" McCade shouted,

stepping an inch closer than before, toe-to-toe and nose-to-nose with Colin. "Are you ready to get married? It's a simple question, young man."

"And I," Colin said through gritted teeth, frantically pulling for answers as to why he was getting such a grazing at this late hour, "have a simple answer. I *am* ready to marry your daughter, sir."

McCade seemed vaguely appeased and took a step backward. "Good answer. Now, I want you to tell me one more thing."

"What is the point of all this?" Colin demanded, slacking away from his military posture and putting some distance between himself and the crazy sergeant. If it weren't for his love for Holly, he would be thinking twice before marrying into a military family.

He jammed his fingers into his hair, and then realized what he'd done. With a frown, he picked up a brush from a nearby table and brushed his tousled hair back into place. "Why are you acting like the Inquisition when you know as well as I do that in less than fifteen minutes I'm going to walk out that door and meet Holly at the altar?"

"When was the last time you told my daughter you loved her?" Sergeant McCade asked, his voice soft, but retaining its usual gruff quality.

"I told I loved her when—well, I—I—" Colin stammered to a halt.

When *had* he said the words? His face flaming with guilt as he realized his oversight.

His *major* oversight.

"Oh, boy," he squeaked, jamming his fingers back through the tips of his hair again.

"Uh-huh," his future father-in-law agreed. "I'd say. It's just as I thought."

"Well, why didn't you say something earlier?" Colin snapped, then cleared his throat against the high-pitched sounds that kept coming from his mouth. His voice was taking on the tone of an adolescent boy.

"I've got to *fix* the problem."

But *how* was he going to fix the problem? His heart pounded against his chest. A cold sweat formed on his forehead.

"Don't think of it as a problem, son," Sergeant McCade advised, patting him awkwardly on the shoulder. "Instead, try to think of it as the building site of a future solution."

At first Colin stared blankly down at his future father-in-law. What was that line of philosophical prose, delivered with equal doses of drill sergeant gruffness and efficiency, supposed to mean?

Love.

Of course. Love was his problem—or rather, the fact that he hadn't actually mentioned the *word* love was the problem.

But love—the emotional candor he felt in his heart

and had obviously not communicated to Holly and the world—was the...how did the sergeant put it?

The building site of a future solution.

"Where's Holly right now?" he asked, sounding every bit as gruff as Ian.

"That's my boy," the sergeant commended. "First hall to your right, two doors down."

"Can you watch Jared for a moment?"

Gramps, as Jared called him, was already sitting down at the puzzle, muttering quietly under his breath about how small they made puzzle pieces these days.

Colin took a moment to straighten his uniform and brush his hair. He'd already blown one proposal. He wasn't going to let a single detail go unnoticed this time around.

Never mind the big ones.

How must Holly be feeling? She was preparing to marry him with no assurance of his love. He couldn't even fathom why she would do such a thing.

She was a brave woman. Crazy, but brave.

He'd have to remember to tell her so.

Holly took a deep breath and sighed. Colin had taken her ultimatums about children and family surprisingly well for a man who claimed he didn't ever want to be saddled with either; but the happiness she expected to feel at winning that argument had somehow got lost in the translation.

The texture of the tea-length white satin wedding

dress brushing against the sides of her calves wasn't quite what she expected. She'd imagined this moment a hundred times as a little girl. Now none of it seemed to be measuring up.

Not even looking in the mirror satisfied her, seeing in her reflection lace, ruffles, a bustle and a great big...*frown.*

Bittersweet longing pooled in her heart. Today she was getting married to the man she loved with all her heart and strength and soul.

This wasn't how it was supposed to be.

Her mother, crouched by her on the floor trying to mend a hem before the big moment, mumbled through the pins she held in her teeth, something about staying in one spot before the dress tore or Holly would end up with satin pinned to her ankle.

With effort and an inward sigh, Holly stopped her restless movement and forced herself to be calm and patient, at least on the outside.

Patience was a trait she'd no doubt have to develop, she thought wryly. She'd be needing a lot of strength and fortitude before this day was out.

And she was looking at a whole lifetime.

The odd thing was, she'd gotten beyond her doubts. Her mind and her heart were completely at ease. She was convinced she was doing the right thing.

She had no qualms about the time it would take to raise Jared. In many ways she was looking forward to becoming an instant mother.

It was instant *wife* that was bothering her at the moment.

"Holly, if you don't stand still, this hem is going to look like a roller-coaster ride."

"Sorry, Mom." She fidgeted unconsciously, and her mother sighed and rolled her eyes.

"Sorry," she said again. She set her jaw and focused all her energy on standing still.

After a few minutes, she'd finally managed to level out her breathing and stop her feet from shifting. She'd even been able to engage in a bit of casual, insubstantial small talk with her mother, who was busy sewing up the final hem.

"All finished," Gwen announced after what seemed like forever. "Why don't you spin around for me? When you were a little girl, that was always the first thing you used to do when you got a new dress—spin around in it to see if it floated."

Holly glanced down at her mother, sharing the moment of nostalgia. Her throat tightened and tears pricked at her eyes.

She remembered.

"Go ahead," her mother urged when she didn't move. "I'll just bet this dress floats like a cloud."

Holly laughed despite herself. Time had proven she was no fairy or a princess, but she didn't see any harm in reliving one whimsical moment. Her dreams of a knight in shining armor had turned into more of a white knightmare, but that didn't mean she couldn't have a little fun this one last time.

She lifted her arms, determined to give her best spin for her mother's sake.

Instead, she spun herself right into Colin's waiting arms. He hooted his appreciation for her effort.

"Colin Brockman, you get out of here this minute!" her mother admonished with a shriek. "You can't see your bride on her wedding day!"

"I need a minute, Mom," he said, grasping Holly around the waist and sweeping her around. "I promise I won't look."

He grinned down at Holly, his eyes sparkling. It was clear he'd already taken a peek, and his gaze told her he liked what he saw.

Well, she had that, anyway. There was nothing conventional about this wedding, anyway. What was one more break with tradition?

Her mother stood and pressed her hands to her hips, her stance belied by a big smile. "It's very unconventional, young man, but I suppose I can give you a minute."

Colin beamed.

"A *minute*," she warned. "No more."

As soon as her mother exited, Holly pried Colin's hands from her waist and held them in front of her, putting a little space between them. She couldn't think when he stood so near her, especially all decked out in his dress whites.

He was an attractive man in any attire, but he was so strikingly handsome in his navy uniform he took her breath away.

"What do you want?" she asked, hoping her voice didn't sound squeaky or hoarse.

He took a step back and brought her hands to his lips, pressing multiple small kisses onto her knuckles. "You look absolutely stunning."

She chuckled despite herself. "You aren't supposed to be looking, remember. And you haven't answered my question."

"Have I told you lately that I love you?"

Her heart bolted to life, though she hastily coaxed it back into its cave. Colin, she reminded herself, often said things off the cuff, things he didn't think about before he spoke.

He'd never intentionally try to hurt someone with his words, of course. He was too good a man for that.

But sometimes he did hurt someone, just the same. He had hurt someone. Hurt her. He'd scarred her heart with his words—or rather, his lack of words.

"You came in here to quote song lyrics to me?" she asked, hoping she sounded light and casual, and hoping she could find something else to think about on her wedding day other than the fact that her future husband didn't love her. This was going to be harder than she'd thought it would be.

He looked taken aback for a minute, and then he

grinned, as if suddenly getting the joke. "I'm a man on a mission."

"I hope so," Holly retorted, "or you're going to have my mother to contend with."

He held up his hands. "Don't scare me."

He paused for a moment, then caught in a breath and pulled her back into his arms before she could step away. His expression was as serious as she'd ever seen it, even more so than on the day of Jared's hearing. It made her nervous when he looked at her like that.

"Do you love me?" he rumbled from the back of his throat.

She nearly choked. "What kind of a question is that? I'm marrying you, aren't I?"

"That's not what I asked," he reminded her gently. "I asked you if you love me."

The dam burst, and all of Holly's pain and insecurity, feelings she'd been repressing and refused to deal with, rose to the surface, spilling over in her tears and in her voice.

"Colin Brockman, how dare you ask me such a thing. I've loved you since the first day I looked up into the top of the school auditorium and saw a thatch-haired thirty-year-old with mischief in his eyes causing trouble in my class."

"Yes. I'm a troublemaker. But do you love me? How do you love me?"

Holly laughed despite herself. "Let me count the ways."

He grinned, but his eyes were no less earnest than before. "Because…?" he prompted.

She shook her head and sighed dramatically. "Oh, all right. I love you for the way you are with Jared, so kind and supportive, always knowing what to say and do. I love that you make him laugh, and the way that you make *me* laugh.

"I love the way you smile at your cat. I love the way you walk. The way you talk. The way you brush your fingers through your hair so it stands on end."

She wiped her wet cheeks with the palm of her hand and chuckled throatily. "Yes…well. I love you. I think you get the picture. Is that what you were looking for? Or should I go on?"

Colin's smile was like sunshine. "I'll take the short version," he teased.

"But you better be ready for the long one," she threatened boldly, laying a hand on his chest, "because you're about to commit to a good, long lifetime of hearing it from me."

He reached up a hand and stroked her cheek, using first the back, and then the tips of his fingers. "I was hoping you'd say that," he said huskily, caressing her jaw with his palm. "Because I love you, Holly McCade-soon-to-be-Brockman, enough to want to marry you, have a dozen kids with you and watch us grow into a couple of old fogies together."

Holly closed her eyes, savoring the sweet words. She'd waited all her life for this moment. But there was still a lingering question.

"Why didn't you tell me you loved me before? Like when you asked me to marry you?" she asked huskily.

"Because I'm an idiot."

She chuckled. "I won't argue. But I think there's more to it than that."

"More to it, how? Holly, don't read a bunch of psychology into it where there isn't any. I just don't always know how to say what I'm feeling. I'm a guy. Cut me some slack."

That might be all there was to it. But even if he meant what he said—and he *was* pretty convincing— there was still something standing between them.

"There's still a lot that's left unsaid between us," she reminded him. "A lot we have never finished discussing."

"There's nothing you can say that will make me take back my words," he assured her. "Or my love."

"Nothing? Weren't you listening to me that day you proposed to me out in my parents' stable? I told you all about my past that day, remember? I was desperate for love, and I—"

Colin cut her off with a kiss.

When he raised his head, she tried again. "Colin, I'm serious. You need to know about the things I did back then and how I—"

Again, he cut her off with a kiss.

"I don't need to know any more than you've already told me," he muttered, nibbling on her bottom lip and spreading kisses down her jaw. "What's in the past is between you and God. I'm sure you've made your peace with Him, and that's all that matters."

He deepened the kiss for a moment, then backed off again. "I'm not looking back. Only forward."

"Yes, but I—"

He laughed, his eyes shining as he bent his head in for another kiss. "If you don't stop talking, we're never going to make it down the aisle today."

She joined in his laughter and kissed his cheek, which was smooth and clean-shaven.

"I love you," he said again, cupping her cheek with his palm. "And I've obviously not said it enough. Believe me when I say I'm going to spend a lifetime making sure you hear it each and every day."

He kissed her again. "I love you."

All her fears and anxiety melted with those three little words. As shaky about herself and her life as she'd been a moment ago, that was as sure as she was now that Colin meant what he said.

It was funny how she only needed to hear the words aloud to know it was true. He'd been showing her all along, if only she'd bothered to listen to what he was telling her with his actions and his heart.

She turned her face into his hand and kissed his

palm. "Until today," she reminded him, "you haven't said *it* at all, you big lug."

He grimaced. "I was afraid of that."

Holly chuckled. "I thought it was a rather large omission, myself."

"That's an understatement. I can't believe you never said anything. Or at least hit me over the head with your attaché. But you're a wonderful woman to let me off the hook so easily."

She arched a brow and smiled. "Who said I'm letting you off the hook, sailor?"

His eyebrows shot up. "Yeah? So what do you say to a big dope who doesn't have the sense to tell the amazing and wonderful woman he loves that she means the world to him?"

Holly slipped her arms around his waist and locked her fingers behind him. The intensity of his gaze matched the sharp intake of his breath. He wrapped his arms around her and held her close to his chest where she could hear the fierce rhythm of his heart.

This, she thought, was exactly where she wanted to be, and this is exactly where she wanted Colin— locked in her arms.

He leaned his face down into her hair and groaned. "What do you say to the idiot who forgot those three crucial little words—*I love you?*" he whispered raggedly.

She smiled, happier in this one moment than she'd ever been. "I do?"

* * * * *

Dear Reader,

Christmas is one of my favorite times of year, as we, God's children, reflect back on the precious birth of our Savior, and look forward to when He will come again in glory. In heaven, there will be no pain, no anxiety and no tears.

In the meantime, we live in a world where mistakes and misunderstandings happen all the time. As Colin did with Holly, sometimes we, or those we love, say and do the wrong things—or say nothing at all. I don't know how many times I've misread a loved one's signal, or jumped to a false conclusion. How wonderful that our God is a God of forgiveness, and He uses our mistakes and sins for our good and His glory. Hallelujah!

On another note—Kids Hope, Inc., is a real, wonderful program through which individual churches and organizations can make a difference in their community schools by mentoring one child at a time. If you'd like more information, you can contact Kid's Hope USA at:
P.O. Box 2517
Holland, Michigan 49422-2517,
or at http://kidshopeusa.gospelcom.net/

Do you have a comment or a prayer request? Write me at: P.O. Box 28140 #16, Lakewood, CO 80228-3108

Happy holidays!

Deb Kastner

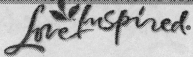

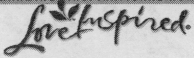